Praise for Roger Croft

Warehouse of Souls

Warehouse of Souls is a solidly constructed page-turner with an ending that will surprise readers. The prose here is very good. The author's descriptions and scenes, while some passages may be overwritten, readers won't be bothered as the action heats up and they keep turning pages.

Though the premise here is nothing new [the hunt for a traitorous double agent], the author makes both the plot and the characters fresh.

Croft's characters are carefully crafted with flaws and redeeming features. Fans of the genre will love Michael Vaux.

A page turner with an ending that comes as a complete surprise.

[*Publishers Weekly, BookLife Prize*]

Solid writing. Good plotting. Reasonably good pace.... the first three books of the author's Mideast spy trilogy should be read in order to make sense [of *Warehouse of Souls*]. But the books should be read. Good series. [*Spy Gals and Guys*]

An espionage tale with believable characters that draw readers into the action.

[*Kirkus Reviews*]

Operation Saladin

Croft's world of double-dealing and treachery, with a suggestion of indifferent, manipulative bureaucrats, confirms the dour observation of a veteran spymaster that loyalty among spies verges on being an oxymoron.... Croft's moral wilderness and compilation of treachery ring far truer than the glamour of James Bond. And the clash between romance, personal loyalty, and institutional duplicity bears the unmistakable tone of one who knows.

[*Publishers Weekly, Starred Review*]

Operation Saladin is an amusing read and may please fans of the spy genre, particularly those who take the professionalism of the Secret Services with a pinch of salt. One thing Croft does well is character study.

[*Daily Star*, Beirut]

Our protagonist Michael Vaux is not a career intelligence officer—he's a retired journalist, independent-minded, and seemingly never without a drink in his hand.... The plot is elaborate and takes the reader down countless blind alleys.... But the reader would be hard-pressed to foresee the final outcome.

[*Egyptian Gazette*, Cairo]

The Maghreb Conspiracy

Vaux rejoins the murky, tense world of chasing shadows and hunting terrorists and soon discovers that this new operation is far more threatening.... Woven with historical fact and modern conflict, Vaux's triumphant return for one last nail-biting mission proves to be a rewarding and satisfying end to the trilogy. Readers who appreciated the rumpled and unlikely hero before, will celebrate his latest success and the deftness with which he bests his enemies ... a likeable, admirable hero who carries a complicated plot with aplomb.

[*Kirkus Reviews*]

Croft's interest in regional politics here plays second fiddle to the tangled web of communications between secret agents, some of whom are playing a double or even triple game.

The book paints an unflattering portrait of Morocco's monarchy, the militant Islamists trying to overthrow it and the Americans supporting it ... an easy and enjoyable read.

[*India Stroughton, Daily Star*, Beirut]

Croft's style of writing is perfectly matched to the rhythm of a good spy novel ... he moves along at a good, solid pace.

[*San Francisco Book Review*]

THE
ALGERIAN
HOAX

A New Michael Vaux Novel

ROGER CROFT

ARCHWAY
PUBLISHING

Archway Publishing books may be ordered through booksellers or by contacting:

Archway Publishing
1663 Liberty Drive
Bloomington, IN 47403
www.archwaypublishing.com
1 (888) 242-5904

Because of the dynamic nature of the Internet, any web addresses or links contained in this book may have changed since publication and may no longer be valid. The views expressed in this work are solely those of the author and do not necessarily reflect the views of the publisher, and the publisher hereby disclaims any responsibility for them.

Any people depicted in stock imagery provided by Getty Images are models, and such images are being used for illustrative purposes only. Certain stock imagery © Getty Images.

ISBN: 978-1-4808-9189-0 (sc)
ISBN: 978-1-4808-9190-6 (hc)
ISBN: 978-1-4808-9188-3 (e)

Library of Congress Control Number: 2020912480

Print information available on the last page.

Archway Publishing rev. date: 10/26/2020

To my nephew Alex Croft
[1986–2018]

Other Books by Roger Croft

The Mideast Spy Quartet:
The Wayward Spy
Operation Saladin
The Maghreb Conspiracy
Warehouse of Souls
Bent Triangle

Nonfiction
Swindle!

Remember that all tricks are either knavish or childish.

—Samuel Johnson [1709–1784]

Author's Note

Construction began on Algiers' Djamaa el Djazair mosque in 2015 and was completed on schedule in 2019. The mosque, the third biggest in the world after Mecca and Medina, was designed by German architects and built by a Chinese construction company.

Chapter 1

WATFORD HEATH, ENGLAND
SEPTEMBER 2015

S he was at the bar again. Michael Vaux watched as she tossed back her shoulder-length, light-brown hair and smiled, as she did often, with her burgundy lips exposing perfect teeth. He knew he had to introduce himself this time.

Without comment, Flory, landlady of the Pig & Whistle, plunked his Cutty Sark down on the scarred, ancient oak bar. It was a double, and he gulped it down to disguise his obvious move as spontaneity: 'We must be neighbors,' he said. 'I've seen you here several times.'

The predictable effort seemed to amuse her, and her opal-blue eyes became iridescent. 'Actually, no. I'm just house-sitting for a friend who lives close by. I live in Hampstead.'

'Oh, I see.' Vaux feared he had lost the initiative along with his rehearsed remarks about the neighborhood and his long attachment to it.

She helpfully broke the silence. 'But I do like the area. Have you lived here long?' She smiled, and Vaux read welcome in the widening of her striking blue eyes.

They exchanged names. Hers was Angela Morris. She said she was a management consultant in the city. Her offices were situated close to the Tower of London. While she was house-sitting here, she took the M1 into London each morning and then back again at night. Her car, he later learned, was a Jaguar XF.

Vaux spoke vaguely about his own life: a long stint in journalism at various news outlets covering international events. He left unmentioned his career since then, the occasional gigs on behalf of Her Majesty's Secret Service.

Flory, catching snippets of the conversation, was keen as always to smooth the way for budding romances, especially if nurtured and lubricated by ample supplies of booze. She sensed that the long absence of Anne, Vaux's long-standing live-in partner, had finally driven this handsome man to ferret out more convenient companions.

What Vaux sensed was inevitable duly came to pass. Two hours later, he and Angela left the crowded, noisy pub and walked arm in arm through the balmy evening to his bungalow, still chatting away about their lives. He was double her age, he guessed, but she seemed to have had a longish and interesting career since graduating in management studies from UCL. A passing stranger would have thought they had known each other forever. They shared the same ironic and irreverent sense of humour—or so it seemed to Vaux—and they were still laughing together as she threw off her strappy stiletto shoes and asked if she could have a coffee.

Later, they made quiet, delicate love and then fell into a deep sleep. At 7 a.m., Vaux's alarm shrilled. He stared at the ceiling as he struggled to gather his thoughts—then he realised someone else was sharing his bed. He felt the warm, silky body that lay beside him. Then he remembered the doctor's appointment.

'Sorry, I've a date with my doctor—canceled the last three times, so I really must do it this time.'

She groaned and said she had a terrible headache. Would he mind if she stayed for another hour or two?

'Not at all,' said Vaux. 'Let yourself out when you want. Just bang the front door closed. See you around, then.'

* * *

Angela Morris heard his car start up and listened intently for telltale noises that would indicate any other presence in the house. The silence was broken only by birdsong and the clatter of neighbors' garage doors. She sighed with relief that her little gamble had paid off: she had found out about the doctor's appointment for that morning from a local field agent, and she had counted on Vaux taking off early so she could ask for a little lie-in.

She got up, shrugged on a terry robe Vaux had left on the bed, and went to the big room where french windows looked out on the long unkempt garden and the rolling countryside beyond. She slipped the encrypted BlackBerry from her black Michael Kors handbag and punched the seven contact numbers.

'Yes,' said a voice she recognized.

'I'm here alone. Bring the boys along. We have about two hours.'

'There in five minutes.'

She had a quick shower in Vaux's ultramodern white-tiled wet room and was vigorously toweling herself when she heard the gentle knocks at the front door. She pulled on her jeans, grabbed one of Vaux's shirts that hung conveniently in a bedroom closet, and hurried to the front door.

The cyber-tech team arrived in two undercover vehicles: an unmarked Land Rover Defender and a faux-Google Street View car adorned with an ungainly roof camera and garish yellow and green stripes.

The burly man who stood at the door smiled broadly and

shook her hand. 'I'm George. We've met before. Are we ready to go?'

'Hi. Yes, I recognized your voice. Angela. Okay, let's do it. But I don't have to tell you, time is of the essence. The target will be back in about an hour.' She hadn't the faintest idea when Vaux would be back, but she wanted to get this whole miserable business over and done with.

'Worse comes to worst, he'll think it's Google making the rounds,' said George. Angela could see three more men looming in the driveway. They carried small leather bags as they entered and spread out into the house.

She was surprised how quickly the cyber operatives had got there. 'Where were you guys waiting?'

'Behind the pub. There's a parking area.'

'Yes, I know. That's where I left my car.'

'We arrived about 3 a.m. Drinking coffee and smoking ever since. We'll be done soon.'

She went in the kitchen and thought about making tea for the boys. She searched for Vaux's tea caddy but then thought better of it. Against all her training. She didn't have time to erase evidence of a home invasion that would trigger Vaux's suspicions—and she had no doubt that somebody who had worked for MI6 would have absorbed into his core being its institutional paranoia of doubt and mistrust. She had noticed during the evening's long conversation how he would occasionally pop leading, pointed questions about her life and career as if he could never shake off his innate suspicions.

There was little talk among the technicians. She heard George suggest certain locations for the listening devices they were planting. They found unlikely places that satisfied the need for secrecy. All the bedrooms were covered, and in the large living room, several pinhole cameras were placed atop the tall window frames and doorjambs. In the bedroom, a miniature mike the size of a US dime was placed securely on the dusty top of Vaux's tall mahogany wardrobe.

After a quick twenty minutes, the three men who had come in the Google Street View car left silently. George got into his Land Rover and smiled again as he gave a finger-to-forehead salute of farewell. 'You looked after the mobile?'

'Yes, in the dead of night when he was in a deep alcoholic blackout.'

'Great. We're leaving the GPS tracker for you. It's on the Welsh dresser in the kitchen.'

She was puzzled by this and a little angry. 'But when will I have the opportunity to do that?'

'Aren't you getting together with him again?'

'It's hardly necessary, is it? Mission accomplished, as far as I'm concerned.'

'Okay, leave it to me. I know his car—a Ford Mondeo. I'll come during the night or fix it when he parks behind the pub—which he does quite often.' He went back into the house, retrieved the GPS, and returned to his car. He gave another salute as he drove away.

Angela breathed a sigh of relief. She really didn't want to see Michael Vaux again.

An hour later, she left Vaux's residence on Willow Drive. She took a look across the street at the bungalow where Vaux's mother had lived and where he said he had grown up. Sheer white curtains covered the windows, and she thought she saw a slight movement at one window as she walked down the gravel driveway. Ten minutes later, she was sitting in her red Jaguar XF and silently saying goodbye—she hoped for the last time—to the Pig & Whistle.

* * *

When Vaux got back from his medical—his doctor had prescribed Norvask for high blood pressure—he checked the bedroom to see if Angela had perhaps decided to sleep in. But she was gone, the bed unmade. A note perhaps, confessing her undying love or at least to say she had enjoyed the evening—but no. Nothing, no traces whatsoever. She'd probably call him later, he thought. But had he given her his phone number? He couldn't remember. He had a landline and kept his Apple 6s with him at all times. He pulled the mobile phone out of his jacket side pocket, but there were no missed calls. He made himself a spicy bloody Mary, went through to the living room, opened the french windows, and sat beside the bistro table on the flag-stoned patio. He looked into the distance—always, for him, a nostalgic but comforting view of the chequered corn fields and hedgerows where a lifetime ago, he grew up and played with the neighborhood kids.

Chapter 2

LONDON, ENGLAND

Patrick Thursfield, thirty-two, fresh out of Ft. Monckton, MI6's training school near Portsmouth, with a degree in medieval and ancient history from Manchester University under his belt, once again reviewed the presentation he was to make within the hour. He had been assigned the challenging task ten days earlier. He was nervous, his palms were wet, and perspiration poured from his armpits. The damp splotches on his crisp white shirt were thankfully hidden by his Austin Read charcoal grey jacket.

His appointment with Alan Craw, deputy director of Department B3, a subgroup of MI6's Mideast and North Africa Desk, was for 10 a.m., and he decided to walk from Vauxhall Cross, MI6's fortress-like headquarters on the South Bank of the Thames, to the rundown offices assigned to B3's personnel on Gower Street, across the river in Bloomsbury. He thought the long walk would calm his anxieties. His sharpened instincts told him that the message he was about to deliver was a bombshell and would cause a reverberation throughout the venerable service to which he had now dedicated his life.

It was an old Georgian building: sash windows, red brick, and a gloomy demeanor, even on a bright sunny day. He observed the tarnished brass plate he had been told to look out for and took the narrow, wobbly lift up to the fourth floor, where Acme Global Consultants Ltd. plied its clandestine trade.

After formal introductions and the obligatory handshakes, Thursfield found himself in a small cluttered office with one grimy window that looked out to the white-tiled internal well of the building. He sat opposite a gloomy, Buddha-like Sir Nigel Adair, deputy director of MI6 and head of B3. Alan Craw, Adair's reedy deputy, sat beside him on an upright Bentwood chair that creaked as Craw rocked forward and backward while listening carefully to Thursfield's brief but seemingly conclusive summary of the recent special internal inquiry.

An enigmatic silence ensued. The quiet was disturbed only by the steady hum of London's traffic, punctuated by an intermittent coo-roo from a fat grey pigeon that had just landed on the external windowsill.

Sir Nigel had put on his round tortoiseshell glasses and stretched his hand out to indicate his desire to hold the one-sheet briefing document. He snatched it from Thursfield's hands as if he felt he had to read it himself to confirm its shocking contents. Craw slid his chair back, perhaps to protect himself from a strong blast of denial or disbelief. Clearly, by implication, his own judgements had been called into question as seriously as those of Sir Nigel's. Indeed, the whole raison d'être of B3—a maverick group of freelance operators willing to cut corners and defy conventional tradecraft to get the job done—was up for a radical reappraisal.

'You expect me to seriously believe that for the last ten years or so, this man Vaux has hoodwinked us, led us up the bloody garden path— several garden paths—deceived us, betrayed us, taken our money, and laughed all the way to the bank and his ill-deserved retirement?'

'I'm afraid it rather looks that way, sir,' Thursfield said apologetically.

'I can't believe it. I simply can't believe it. In fact, I'd go so far as to say I *don't* believe it. What say you, Craw?'

Craw summoned his not-inconsiderable powers, nurtured at Oxford Union debates of some decades ago, to answer Sir Nigel's rhetorical question with all the ambiguity he could muster.

'Well, sir, with due respect, Vauxhall's investigative team went to great lengths to be thorough, fair, and unbiased. By that, I mean I saw no evidence of any effort to undermine B3's reputation or overall trustworthiness, loyalty, etc....'

'Absolute bunk,' Sir Nigel roared, prompting Thursfield to push back on his wheeled Warminster chair in a futile attempt to escape Sir Nigel's wrath.

Sir Nigel continued, 'I'm damned if I'm going to accept these findings hook, line, and sinker. These people at Vauxhall were never on our team. For years, they've been envious of our many breakthroughs and successes, most of which, in one way or another, Vaux contributed to and helped immeasurably.'

'Yes, sir. But that's the point. They have apparently concluded that the evidence against Vaux is immense; and they therefore contend that we have been remiss and negligent in employing that man and endorsing his judgements.'

Sir Nigel detected Craw's usual ambivalence when bureaucratic conflicts threatened his career goals. '"*That* man?" Why, he was one of our most effective operatives—even if he was hired as a nonofficial cover officer. He was one of the best of what we used to call the Occasionals. For heaven's sake, he retired after a successful career in the news business. Why the hell did he need us? It's not as if he suddenly appeared as a walk-in. *We* suborned *him* to help us because he offered great cover and terrific experience in the areas that are our remit—the Middle East and North Africa.'

Thursfield, uncomfortable at the unfamiliar sight of two of the service's senior officers at each other's throats, now thought it diplomatic to make a move. He stood up, put a beige folder under his arm, and was about to diplomatically announce his departure for HQ when he heard Sir Nigel order him to sit bloody well down until the two men from Department B3 had finished discussing what appeared to be an inevitable crisis.

A long, tense silence ensued, during which Sir Nigel's lips moved almost imperceptibly; his bushy grey-black eyebrows rose and fell as he read and reread the summary of charges against Michael Vaux in the wake of a special internal investigation into Vaux's B3 assignments, stretching back to the 1990s.

Thursfield fidgeted and began to roll his chair towards Sir Nigel's desk and then retreated in an unconscious rhythmic motion, perhaps designed to quell his anxieties. He waited for Sir Nigel's summation and his hoped-for dismissal.

Sir Nigel finally took off his glasses. Craw put out his hand for the one-page document. 'I'll get it photocopied right away, sir. Will three copies suffice?'

'Get a dozen while you're at it. We'll need to contact and talk to a number of staffers and former agents. That's if we intend to build up some defense for poor old Vaux.'

Craw glanced at Thursfield, whose eyes widened to signal a meeting of the minds over the dubious task of defending a man accused of treachery, deceit, and cowardly malfeasance.

Sir Nigel said, 'You do realise, Craw, that they are saying Vaux was a plant, recruited by my predecessor, Sir Walter Mason, and aided and abetted by you, yourself, back in the years. You'll have some explaining to do if and when Vaux comes up for a *sub camera* trial for treason.'

'Aren't we jumping the gun here, sir? I'm sure there are explanations for all this—'

'Read the bloody memorandum. They claim Vaux was put up to volunteering to work for us by Syria's secret intelligence service—the GSD, no less. Sir Walter, God rest his soul, hired Vaux, and you, may I remind you, were Sir Walter's deputy then, as you are now mine. You'll have to come up with some answers, my boy.'

Sir Nigel assumed a somewhat complacent look. The ball was now in Craw's court.

But he had apparently decided on an aggressive defense. 'I remember it as if it were yesterday. These people are wrong, dead wrong, sir. For starters, Vaux was hooked by the undercover recruiting team at head office—you know, those pale, inoffensive little people who hang out, or used to, in the sub-basement of Century House.

'They discovered he was an old friend of Syria's chief armaments buyer, a man named Ahmed Kadri, if memory serves. Vaux and Kadri were at university together—Bristol, I think—and they carried on an on-again/off-again relationship for many years. We used Vaux in Operation Helvetia—a successful caper which resulted in our getting all the dope on Syria's planned arms build-up.'

Sir Nigel looked dubious. 'Yes, but didn't we suspect even then that Vaux deliberately downsized the plans for a Syrian arms build-up to help Kadri curry favour with Assad?'

'Yes, but Vaux then relented and gave us the full bill of goods. We excused his earlier deception; put it down to old loyalties and all that.'

Sir Nigel said, 'Then there's the charge that this Palestinian walk-in, one Alena Hussein, who later defected to Syria, had an affair with Vaux while they both worked for B3. She apparently convinced him of the righteousness of the Arab cause.'

Craw felt compelled to go public on his preferred version of the institutional history. 'Yes, but a few years later, Syria's intelligence chiefs then suspected that Vaux's loyalties were to the Brits, and he was in fact working undercover for British intelligence. They figured his mission was to compromise and undermine Alena, who had become GSD's station chief in Cairo at the time Vaux was doing another journalism gig there. The Damascus-based newspaper Vaux worked for called him back to Syria, and Alena, his lover, warned him that it was a trap. If he returned, he'd be subject to a staged trial and probably a death sentence.'

Sir Nigel said, 'There's much more to it than just the Cairo affair. They're saying he was in cahoots with AQIM, Al-Qaeda in the Islamic Maghreb, for God's sake. His heroics in Morocco, when he rescued young Micklethwait from the clutches of AQIM, was, according to their findings again, a put-up job, a deception, to convince us that he would risk his own life in that final shoot-out to rescue poor Micklethwait.'

Listening to the abstruse debate, Thursfield's roundish face betrayed a look of bewilderment.

Sir Nigel elaborated, 'Micklethwait was one of our best young operatives. He was later killed in Beirut by those Hezbollah thugs while on a mission with Vaux to hunt down a mole working out of the British embassy.'

'Another one of Vaux's successful missions, I would add,' said Craw, now sensing it might be expedient—despite his long-enduring antipathy towards Vaux—to express his own scepticism about the internal inquiry's findings.

Sir Nigel glanced quickly at his gold Patek Philippe wristwatch, stood up, pushed his ancient leather chair back against the wall, and declared he must not be late for lunch with Lady Adair at the Savoy's River Room. The meeting was over.

'Read and inwardly digest, as my old housemaster used to say,' Sir Nigel said as he handed Craw the memorandum.

* * *

TOP SECRET

From: TARBOOSH
To: Internal Special Inquiry re WESTROPP/V.
OPERATION HELVETIA, 1992

Location: Geneva, Mideast Peace Conference

> *Task: to uncover details of Syria's multibillion-dollar arms deal with Russia.*

Agent in place: Vaux. Code name: Derek Westropp.

> *Bio check: B3's back-up plan to recruit Vaux involved romantic entanglement with B3 agent BARBARA BOYD [aka VERONICA BELMONT] who posed as PhD researcher when she made contact with Vaux at his local pub.*

> *Syrian delegation headed by Ahmed Kadri, Syria's chief arms negotiator and an old university friend of WESTROPP/V.*

> *Investigative findings: BB [born: Alena Hussein] recruited earlier by MI6/B3 as a vetted walk-in. Fluent in Arabic. Father, a Palestinian MD, trained at UCL HOSPITAL, London.*

> *CHARGE: While in Geneva, BB/VB aided and abetted kidnapping and detention of WESTROPP/V, where he underwent brainwashing sessions at the lakeside Russian consulate. Based on his former friendship with KADRI and his strong affection for BB/VB, he succumbed to their plan to reveal details of a fictitious, much smaller arms deal to WESTROPP/V's handlers at B3. This 'chickenfeed' was accepted by B3 as the genuine article, despite cautionary scepticism from CIA liaison.*

> *CONCLUSION: The false intelligence supplied by WESTROPP/V [now a private UK resident] with the cooperation of double agent BB/VB is tantamount to high treason. BB/VB is now resident in Damascus, where she continues to work for ASSAD'S General Security Directorate [GSD]. Westropp/V resides in Watford, UK. 111XM6B3*

Chapter 3

'Not many people can afford to turn down fifty thousand pounds sterling,' said Craw.

'I can't, either,' said Vaux. 'It's the timing of the thing. I've been patiently waiting for Anne's return, so we can start to rebuild our lives together. She's been gone two years now—save for the odd brief visits—and that's a long time for a man at my age.'

Craw relished his prepared announcement. 'But haven't you heard, old boy?'

'Heard what?'

'She's announced her engagement, to this fellow Bill Soames. They met at the embassy in Berlin—or more accurately, I understand, at the bar of the nearby Adlon Hotel. He's the deputy commercial secretary in our Berlin shop—her boss, actually. They're in the same department: passports, visas, that sort of thing. They've apparently been going together now for ten months or so. Didn't she tell you?'

Vaux said nothing. So this was why she had recently resorted to tourist postcards as the main means of communication and why even they seemed to be getting less and less frequent. His reaction was a blend of dismay and an unfamiliar *frisson* of betrayal.

Like a cat that has struck down a sparrow, Craw then pounced for the kill. 'Does this piece of news perhaps change the landscape somewhat, Vaux? Doesn't the prospect of a new assignment look a tad more attractive? You're a free man now; think of the romantic possibilities. Your first stop will be Nice in the south of France, for God's sake. All those glamorous bikini-clad starlets; think of the romantic possibilities. Need I say more?'

Vaux couldn't think of a sufficiently witty reply. But he knew Craw, a long-time rival for Anne's heart, had enjoyed delivering what he knew would be bad, life-changing news.

Craw suggested, 'Think it over for a few days. We're patient people. We want you for this operation, Vaux. Your experience with the Arabs and knowledge of what's going on in the Middle East—why, you're just the man to fit the bill.'

'Yes,' he said. He pushed himself up from the hard Windsor chair and left Craw scribbling something on a notepad.

Closing the door gently, Vaux looked over to the battered oak desk where Anne used to sit. Her ancient Remington typewriter had been replaced by a desktop computer, behind which a sturdy white-haired lady from the general typing pool sat, her nimble fingers dancing over the keyboard as she closely read the text on the monitor. She looked up at him with a wan smile and a short nod as he walked past her through the shabby hallway to the gloom of the fourth-floor landing and descended slowly in the antique, juddering lift.

* * *

Earlier that day, Sir Nigel had been ordered to attend a one-on-one briefing session with Bill Oxley, a member of Vauxhall's small team of counter-espionage operatives. Sir Nigel considered Oxley below his pay grade, so he told Alan Craw, his deputy, to attend in his place and report back to him later.

Oxley had acquired a reputation among the denizens of Whitehall's intelligence community for the stolid, persistent pursuit of deep-cover moles and unsuspected double agents. Usually, the offenders were let go without fuss, their accumulated pension rights suspended, their denials ignored. Oxley, now in his early sixties, had served his apprenticeship as a young recruit assigned to the small team of spy-catchers who exposed veteran KGB agent Colonel Oleg Gordievski, who was later turned into one of Britain's most successful and productive double agents [Note 1].

Among his other notable scores: the exposure of Richard Tomlinson, a career MI6 man, an alumni of Cambridge, who in the last decade of the last century joined the long list of renegades incubated by that esteemed and ancient university [Note 2]. Another coup was the eventual uncovering of former Labour Party leader Michael Foot as an alleged, one-time Soviet asset.

Oxley, grey-blond hair whitening at the temples, a prominent Adam's apple below a long chin and thin nose, was tall and slim, wore tweed suits, and smoked Lucky Strikes, a nostalgic and addictive habit acquired during his probationary Washington posting in the long drawn-out and prolonged aftermath of the Philby-Maclean disaster. [Note 3].

Despite Oxley's reputation, Craw was determined to show no overblown respect for the storied spy catcher. 'I've heard a lot about you, of course,' Craw said. 'But thankfully, we've never crossed paths.'

Never having had previous contact with Oxley, Craw had assumed the mantle of a man beyond reproach.

Oxley, stone-faced, stubbed out his half-smoked Lucky Strike in a large ceramic ashtray. He stretched over to his in-tray and grabbed one sheet of paper. He tossed it over the desk and watched as Craw carefully picked it up while searching his jacket pockets for his half-moon, gold-framed spectacles. He found them on the fourth try in the top pocket. Craw was a slow and meticulous reader [in his teens, he had spent long summer holidays working as a proofreader at a small provincial newspaper], and his audible murmurings were noted by Oxley with some impatience.

TOP SECRET

From: TARBOOSH
To: Internal Special Inquiry re WESTROPP/V.
OPERATION SALADIN, 2000
Location: UK

> TASK: To aid and abet defecting Syrian nuclear scientist.

AGENT IN PLACE: VAUX/WESTROPP assigned as NOC [Non-Official Cover Officer].

> Scenario: While Dr Nessim Said was under Vaux's close guard and general care, the renowned nuclear scientist was assassinated by hit team hired by the Assad regime.

> WESTROPP/V. suspected an Israeli targeted killing along the lines of OPERATION SPHINX [PARIS] in 1980. Israel strongly denies any knowledge of Nessim's planned defection or wish to stay in the UK. Israelis also continue to deny any operations involving extra-judicial assassinations.

> AGENT GERTRUDE [DAMASCUS] confirms MI6's suspicions: Syrian-based hit team entered UK borders without difficulty under false IDs several days prior to the killing of Dr. Said.

> ALENA HUSSEIN contacts Westropp/V. approximately at this time and states desire to redefect to UK along with crown jewels of Syria's battle plans v. Israel; plus up-to-date details of Assad's arms build-up and secret nuclear weapons program.

Motive? Ostensibly her unassuaged love for WESTROPP/V., and perhaps nostalgia for a country which gave her refugee father domicile and education in the UK.

ALENA HUSSEIN re-enters UK under cloak of anonymity, meets Vaux, who does not report meeting to his superiors at B3-MI6.

Post Dr. Nessim's assassination, SYRIA's hit team attempt to kill WESTROPP/V. in safe house. He is with Hussein at the time, and she allegedly falls victim to crossfire between WESTROPP/V.'s guards and group of assassins.

CHARGE: VAUX conspired with known Syrian secret agents to facilitate murder of Dr. SAID, TO PREVENT LATTER FROM DIVULGING MAJOR ELEMENTS OF SYRIA'S NUCLEAR ARMS PROGRAM.

Later attack on safe house probably a ruse to lift suspicions from WESTROPP/V. and cloak his participation in conspiracy.

Conclusion: Along with INTERNAL MEMO 111XM6B3, the facts related above suggest VAUX continued to collude with SYRIAN GOVERNMENT, long after suspicions were aroused in the wake of OPERATION HELVETIA.

112XM6B3

* * *

Vaux scanned the sensational, three-inch-tall headlines of the tabloid *Evening Standard* that proclaimed to its conservative readers that Jeremy Corbyn, an obscure North London politician, had been elected the new leader of the British Labour Party. Without reading the story, he tossed the paper onto the vacant seat opposite [at around 10.30 a.m., the usual commuters were still busy in their offices] and tried to think about how his life, like Corbyn's, had suddenly taken an unforeseen turn. Without Anne, everything had changed. He had always thought he would be with her for the rest of his life; the fact that he was double her age only reinforced his sentimental conviction that she would be his final partner.

He looked out at the grim terraced houses that flashed by as the commuter train left the cramped northern suburbs of London and thought that for once, Craw could be right: A new assignment would perhaps distract him from the bleak knowledge that Anne had apparently had enough. She had met someone of her own age group, and he knew he could never stand in her way. She must follow her heart.

Forty minutes later, in the cobbled forecourt of the red brick, clock-towered Victorian railway station, he clambered into the back of an ancient Austin taxi and asked the driver if he knew the Pig & Whistle pub up on the heath.

'Yes, mate. But I don't think they'll be open yet.'

Vaux looked at his old Accurist watch with the faded face and Roman numerals. It was eleven thirty. 'I think they open at eleven,' he replied.

He was right. He ordered a Heineken from the stranger behind the bar and knew he was headed for what in his youth they called a 'liquid lunch.'

He downed a couple of pints and then left. He walked back to his house, his earlier anguish allayed by alcohol on an empty stomach and by the sudden recall of his evening walk along the same leafy streets some weeks ago with the beautiful Angela Morris. He never heard another word from her. He must be losing his touch, and it again occurred to him that perhaps another jaunt on behalf of Her Majesty's Secret Service was just the sort of stimulant his flagging hormones needed.

But first, he'd give Anne another try. He knew that to call her mobile was a waste of time. She had never become what she called a 'smartphone addict' and had told him firmly that she only used her Apple 6 in an emergency. She never defined what she would view as an emergency, and Vaux never pursued the matter. So he lifted the receiver of the landline, attached to the kitchen wall. He punched in the numbers that he knew by heart.

An English-speaking operator asked him to hold the line while she put his call through to Anne's office. His hopes soared, for this was the first time he had been asked to wait while some efforts were made to locate her. No instant barrier had been erected. Perhaps at last he would get some answers. But the waiting seemed interminable. Then came the music—Johann Strauss's *Blue Danube*, if he wasn't mistaken. The Berlin Symphony Orchestra was soaring to a powerful crescendo when the music suddenly cut off.

'Mr. Vaux?'

'Yes, I'm still here.'

'I'm sorry to have kept you waiting. I'm afraid Anne went home early today with a bad cold. She left instructions to hold any calls and take messages. Sorry about that.'

Vaux hooked the receiver back in its cradle, sighed, and walked through to the living room. He flung open the french windows and stepped out to the flagstone terrace. There was a slight chill in the air. Summer was over—and so, it seemed, was Anne. He sat down at the marble-topped bistro table; a few dead leaves had fallen onto it from the elm that dominated the garden. Autumn approached, and winter not far behind.

His thoughts returned to Anne. Why hadn't she called him? Why had she ignored him? This was completely out of character. She had always been an open, sunny person. If she had suddenly been struck by Cupid's sharp arrow, she surely would have come to him, tearfully confessed all in the hope of his forgiveness and understanding. He now felt miserably guilty of not making a bigger deal of the whole thing. Why hadn't he flown over to Berlin, protested at her prolonged silence, remonstrated as the injured party?

He knew the answer: because he had begun to take their relationship for granted. She had been too young. He had always known that he was old enough to be her father, and therefore, subconsciously, he must have convinced himself that the affair would be idyllic but brief. And that's how it turned out.

His mobile's screen suddenly lit up as it sounded the patriotic chimes of *Rule Britannia*. He didn't recognize the number. 'Please God, let it be Anne,' he muttered as he put the phone close to his ear.

'Hello.'

'Craw here, old boy. Just wondering whether you've thought things over. I don't have to remind you that, as always, time is of the essence.'

More to end the conversation quickly than with any sure conviction, Vaux heard himself reply, 'Yes, all right. I'll give it a go.'

* * *

Angela Morris bent over the monitor, her hand on her colleague's shoulder, reading the latest report from the Surveillance/Intercept Department at MI6'S Vauxhall Cross Headquarters.

'Umm. Just the two tries yesterday at contacting the girlfriend?'

Jim Everest, a wizened, laconic cipher clerk, confirmed her observation by a slight nod. 'But if we go back to the date of your first encounter with our target, he's made a good twenty attempts at all hours of the day and night.'

'What sort of runaround are we giving him exactly?'

'Oh, the usual prevarications. "She's just stepped out. Can we get her to call you back?" Or, "Sorry, she's taken a few days off. The flu, we think."'

A wry smile curled her lips. 'Poor Vaux. He must be tearing his hair out. Any second thoughts on her part?'

'What do you mean?'

'Well, she's not getting cold feet, is she? She may have a crush on this commercial attaché, but she knows she has to toe the line as far as handling Vaux goes.'

'Nah, she's on board. She's been promoted from the secretarial pool at Department B3 and is now a full-fledged assistant deputy commercial officer attached to the Passport Office at the embassy in Berlin. First big step in what she is sure will be a long and distinguished diplomatic career.'

Angela Morris smiled again. 'You're a cynical old bugger, Jim.'

Chapter 4

MARSEILLE, FRANCE

Craw had promised Nice; Marseille was what he got. But Marseille would do, he told himself. A gritty, manic port city that lacked the glamour and opulence of the Riviera but still had the romantic, luminescent charms of an old Roman harbour.

Michael Vaux sat at a table in front of the small café where he was to make contact with a cut-out that, he had been told, would pass on the vital information he needed to launch what had been quickly dubbed Operation Mascara. He thought the name had sprung from one of Craw's sex-related obsessions, until he was sternly rebuked: Mascara, protested Craw, was the name of a small town in northern Algeria.

Vaux wasn't sure if the contact would do a brush-pass, magically delivering the vital info into his hands before disappearing into thin air, or whether there would be a more sophisticated performance that would deliver the required marching orders. It was early morning, so he ordered a croissant and *café crème*.

There were a few solitary men sitting at small marble-topped tables under a white-and-green striped awning on the street-level terrace. He noted the newspapers they scanned—*La Provence, Nice-Matin.* The chain-smoking local butcher, identified by his blood-stained apron, sat behind him like a sentry at the door to the gloomy interior of the café-bar. He seemed to be engrossed in the sports pages of the cumbersome broadsheet, the *New York Times International.* He had noticed him as he sat down and wondered whether this was an unsubtle message from on high, but the heavy, bearded man suddenly got up and left.

After about thirty minutes, Vaux felt the urge to walk away. He recalled vaguely one of the old tradecraft lessons learned at Portsmouth: *if the initial rendezvous fails at first attempt, go to the same place at the same time the next day.* So he decided to repeat the performance the next morning. He asked for *l'addition,* and the proprietor emerged with a long, printed chit. Vaux scanned the numbers and plunked down a ten euro note. Then he saw it: stapled to the bill was an old deleted receipt with handwritten instructions: *Chez Loury, Rue Fortia. 20.00 hrs.*

* * *

Craw's directions had been clear and precise:

"Once contact is made, you are to vacate your five-star hotel and move into the rundown district, south of the Quai de Rive, and act on subsequent instructions."

Vaux guessed that Craw's concession to let him have a few preliminary days of rest at the plush Hotel Dieu was a sop for tougher, less elegant times to come. But past experience suggested they also provided Craw with a tinge of sadistic pleasure at the vision of Vaux having to abandon the sybaritic life to which he had become so easily accustomed. Vaux's lavishly furnished suite looked out to the glittering, baroque Notre Dame basilica, which sat on a hill several miles to the south. While in the immediate foreground, the sun-soaked, ochred sprawl of the old harbor shimmered in the evening heat of a dying summer.

That afternoon, he took a taxi to the Gare St. Charles TGV station and stashed a suitcase full of shirts, pants and shoes plus the spare, four-chambered Sig Sauer P226, into a metal locker whose four-digit code he quickly wrote down on the back page of his false passport.

* * *

Six hundred miles to the north-west, London's busy, crammed streets were being gently washed by a steady, warm drizzle. Umbrellas were unfurled, closed, and shaken as men and women walked briskly to the comforting shelter of coffee houses and offices.

Alan Craw had won a minor bureaucratic battle that morning: instead of obeying Bill Oxley's summons to his claustrophobic fifth-floor bunker [in his assigned base of operations, there were no windows overlooking the murky, majestic Thames], Craw had insisted that Oxley pay at least a one-off visit to the home of Department B3, perhaps to convey some obeisance from on high to the specialist group of MI6 field agents whose maverick, barely legal operations, he would always claim, had produced several storied coups in the field of international espionage.

Shaking the water off his hazel-wood cane umbrella in the dusty foyer of the old Georgian terraced house, Oxley unconsciously adopted an air of disdain as he approached the bronze narrow cage of the lift that took him up to the fourth floor. A few doors down the narrow corridor, he observed the tarnished brass plate that identified the satellite MI6 operation: Acme Global Consultants Ltd. After he entered, he looked down his long nose as he surveyed the foyer and the portly, white-haired lady who sat behind a computer monitor, fingers tapping lightly on the keyboard.

Oxley sat on one of the upright wicker chairs that were lined up as in a doctor's waiting room. Down the crepuscular corridor, Alan Craw sat in his small office, observing the second hand of the non-digital gold Cartier wristwatch a former girlfriend had given him a few birthdays ago. He waited for five long minutes to pass, got up, and prepared to greet the man whose impeccable reputation was undeniable but who would no doubt benefit from the reminder that the not-to-be ignored record of Department B3 sometimes needed to be driven home.

Oxley at last sat down opposite Craw, who now went through the theatrics of tidying his desk, moving old glass ink trays [now cherished as archaic office ornaments] to various positions, picking up a pile of foolscap papers, shaking them every which way, and placing the neat pile on an elegant mahogany credenza, to which he turned on his swivel chair several times.

Oxley waited patiently for Craw to suggest they start the briefing.

'Well now, Bill, what more have you garnered to speed Operation Mascara along the road to fulfillment?' Craw asked, adopting an earnest, avuncular air towards his senior colleague.

'I take it Sir Nigel is otherwise occupied?' Oxley asked, ignoring Craw's specious curiosity.

'Yes, indeed,' said Craw. 'Probably at Harrod's, buying a new hat for Lady Adair. It's her birthday.'

Oxley suppressed his irritation at Craw's deliberately casual attitude. He fully realised that from Craw's point of view, the ongoing in-house inquiry into Michael Vaux's real allegiance was tantamount to censoring his own personal judgement and intelligence skills. So he decided to be brusque and businesslike.

'We understand that contact has been made and that the operation is under way. Everything should go according to plan. We shall have to be somewhat patient, of course. In this sort of caper, a lot can go wrong, unforeseeable things could happen, and the ultimate goal of the operation may well be aborted—depending on the accumulating evidence.'

Craw, who had been buffing his fingernails as Oxley spoke, suddenly looked up. 'Ah! So you are not 100 per cent certain that your original thesis is watertight. Perhaps you embarked on a wild goose chase.'

Oxley smiled. 'You do like to mix your metaphors, don't you? No, I think that's a bit of wishful thinking, old boy. Meanwhile, please read and digest our latest summary of the situation. Copy to Sir Nigel, of course.'

He placed a sheet of paper in front of Craw, who chose to ignore it. Oxley then got up and bid Craw a good day.

* * *

TOP SECRET

FROM: TARBOOSH
TO: Internal Special Inquiry re WESTROPP/V.
OPERATION APOSTATE, 2005
Location: Tangier, Morocco

> *SCENARIO: A senior operative of terrorist group Al-Qaeda in the Islamic Maghreb [AQIM] offered high value intelligence on the group's top membership, recruitment plans, and overall strategies to disrupt the economies and polity of the Maghreb countries [Morocco, Algeria, Libya etc.] Defector wished to remain in place pending clandestine discussions between his envoy, one Mokhtar Tawil, and MI6 in London.*
>
> *Plan was aborted following assassination of Tawil on the Paris-Madrid night train. MI6/B3 agent MICKLETHWAIT ['M'] who had been assigned to accompany Tawil back to Morocco, was ordered to continue to Tangier—pending*

developments and on the chance/hope of meeting up with the defector or his representatives.

Department B3, with Vauxhall in support role, suborned occasional agent WESTROPP/V, who, by happenstance, was vacationing in Tangier at the time, to aid and help 'M' in his endeavours to find and make contact with would-be defector. Within days of his arrival in Tangier, 'M' was kidnapped, presumably by AQIM operatives, in front of the RIF, a well-known nightclub on Tangier's Corniche.

CHARGE: WESTROPP/V, whose anti-Israeli tendencies and pro-Arab sympathies have, over the years, been reported and recognized by various SIS associates and colleagues [including CIA informants], had deliberately informed AQIM operatives of M's presence in Tangier as well as his remit—to contact the traitor/defector in their midst.

CONCLUSION: AQIM held 'M' as a bargaining chip to pressure CIA/AFRICOM to release one ABDUL JUHAYMAN, accused co-conspirator in the 2003 Casablanca terrorist suicide bombings. The blackmail worked, and JUHAYMAN was duly released in exchange for B3's 'M'.

113XM6B3

Chapter 5

Rue Fortia is a narrow cobbled street off the Quai de Rive Neuve, the south bank of the old harbour. Small cramped cafés front shabby five-story dwellings that house families with screaming toddlers, while the upper floors provide unpretentious offices for various venerable trade associations and professionals: above the small, oddly-named L'oeuf Bleu restaurant was the head office of *Syndicate des Pecheurs* [fishermen's union]; while certain *Cabinets Avocats* [lawyers] and *Experts-Comptables* [accountants] shared the upper floors.

Walking south, Vaux came across a small square dominated by a bronze statue of Milon de Crotone, apparently a renowned Cretan wrestler, sculpted by a Monsieur P. Puget in 1850. The tiled plinth, which revealed the statue's identity, was desiccated by age and weather, and offered numerous concealed gaps and dark holes which Vaux thought ideal for a dead-letter drop.

At the junction with Cours Pierre Poujet, he saw it: Chez Loury, an abandoned restaurant. Neglected flower boxes on the sills of the shuttered windows displayed petrified miniature cactus plants and withered flowers. He looked for any sign of life, but except for a scraggy tabby cat prowling the premises, the place was lifeless. The windows of the upper floors were boarded up.

Vaux decided to return to the small room he had earlier paid for at the ironically named Hotel Splendide. It was the sort of place that rented rooms out to couples on an hourly basis. Or for the night, if someone sought a longer respite from the manic streets. The fading skeletal blonde at the desk gave him a key that was attached to a brass object the size of a golf ball. No. 5 on the first floor, overlooking an overgrown, fenced junkyard now apparently colonized by the area's exploding cat population.

Vaux gave a quick glance around the room. His holdall looked as if nobody had touched it since he put it down on the small luggage rack after checking in. The minimal wash basin in the corner reeked of urine, and the bed looked unappetizing: the pillow cases were still stained by the previous occupant, who must have been addicted to brilliantine or hair oil. Similarly, the bed's headboard, made of sickly colored synthetic leather, displayed dark patches where perhaps many heads had rested before the ritual nightly read or smoke.

But he was not yet deterred. He knew his immediate task would determine whether he would stay the night. He threw off the bed's counterpane, peeled off the grey woolen blanket, and closely examined the bed sheets between which he would, if he chose, sleep the night. The test failed: there were greenish and reddish blotches on the bottom sheet, and further down where the edges were tucked in under the spring mattress, an accumulation of pubic hairs and toenail cuttings. The bedbugs had no doubt hastily retreated from their disturbed habitat.

That was it. Vaux left the key at the now abandoned front desk and headed for the nearest half-decent bar. His instinct had told him he had been observed discreetly since he had made a showy inspection of the Chez Loury premises, and he was confident he would soon make the breakthrough contact.

* * *

HAMPSTEAD, LONDON

Oxley bought two brimming pints of bitter and carried them delicately over to the cramped booth that he had managed to claim before the arrival of his junior colleague, Patrick Thursfield. It was nine o'clock on a busy Friday night, and the decibel level was high—which is the way Bill Oxley liked it. He looked forward to the interview—for that's what it was, even though Thursfield had been given the impression that the invitation was merely for a post-workweek social chat with a friendly, if senior, colleague.

Oxley, who had heard a lot about Thursfield's youthful enthusiasm and his love of ancient history, wanted to test the man out for what would be a crucial role in Operation Mascara. He was sceptical of the wave of new talent recruited from the provincial universities and found it hard to believe that this new pan-class generation would be talented enough to perform any better under stress than his own cohorts from Oxbridge. Traitors like Maclean, Burgess, and Philby were ancient history and exceptions to the rule; in his view, the British Secret Service would always have to be run by the traditional establishment, whose sons and daughters, thanks to the public school system, usually wound up at one of the two oldest universities.

Patrick Thursfield slid into the opposite leather bench without a murmur. The two men shook hands over the scarred and stained oak table and winced as they took mutual swigs of the tepid ale. Oxley saw that his colleague had had time to go home and change into casual weekend attire—blazer and blue jeans—which he felt put him in the position of a stuffy senior colleague. He decided to disown the easy label.

'Is it Pat or Patrick, old boy?'

'Oh, Pat's fine. And it's "Bill," I take it.'

'Yes, absolutely.'

They clinked their thick glass tankards together, and Thursfield looked around the crowded bar to see if any of his local friends were performing their usual Friday night rituals.

'I understand you live locally?' Oxley had observed Thursfield's roving examination of the Friday night punters. In particular, he followed the direction of Thursfield's eyes to see what kind of acquaintances he may acknowledge in a pub known for years as a popular venue for local gays. He wasn't against homosexuals, but everyone knew they were more susceptible to blackmail—and therefore a greater security risk—than the average hetero. And scrutiny of Thursfield's personnel file hadn't helped: in the box devoted to Sexual Orientation, the compiler had typed *Undetermined*—a notation Oxley had found ambiguous and quite unhelpful.

But now, Oxley's current assessment of the situation yielded nothing of any interest. Thursfield looked comfortable and relaxed and didn't seem to know anyone or acknowledge any possible acquaintances that might give a clue about his social life.

'I asked you here this evening to discuss a very important proposition, both in relation to your career and how you can help our team in a critical operation.'

Thursfield's eyes widened as he took another quick swig at the warmish ale that had now lost its foamy head.

'In a very few days, you will be sent to Bude, Cornwall. Mean anything to you?'

'Well, I've heard GCHQ has outgrown its quarters in Bletchley and has built a satellite operation there, sir. Apart from that, my family used to holiday in Cornwall every summer. Bude's just up the coast from Padstow, isn't it?'

Oxley ignored this irrelevant question. 'GCHQ's operation in Bude has got nothing to do with their long history of code cracking and monitoring communications between potential enemies—and allies, for that matter. It's a brand-new set-up, designed for this contemporary age. They're into cyberspace—the World Wide Web, hacking communications that increasingly rely on the internet, the dark web, all that stuff.'

'Sounds challenging,' Thursfield said as he wondered whether he sounded sufficiently enthusiastic.

Oxley looked around for potential eavesdroppers. He leaned towards Thursfield so that his muted voice was just audible. 'It's to be called Operation Mascara. You will be going to the south of France to set up a cyber operations base designed to penetrate communications between various terrorist groups operating out of Algeria and North Africa. I'm talking about the likes of Al-Shabaab and Al Qaeda in the Islamic Maghreb, AQIM for short. That's all I can tell you at the moment. Interested?'

Thursfield tried to compose a quick, enthusiastic answer. 'Absolutely, sir.' Technology and the internet had never been his thing, but this was not the time to reveal his shortcomings. 'I've been waiting for a chance to see some action at the sharp end, sir.'

'Good man,' said Oxley.

An awkward silence ensued as Oxley concentrated on Thursfield's eye movements.

'You'll be given your marching orders on Monday morning, 9 a.m. sharp. You know B3's offices; you went there just recently to meet Sir Walter and his deputy Craw.'

'Yes. It was rather an awkward moment, if I remember correctly. I had to deliver the summaries of our investigation into the loyalty of one of B3's veteran agents.'

Oxley was about to say something when Thursfield suddenly jumped up to welcome a slim and pretty girl who had rushed over from the bar. Thursfield and the girl, in yellow sweater and blue jeans, air-kissed several times before he made the introductions.

'This is Olive, Bill. Next-door neighbor, really, aren't you, darling?'

She still stood before them. 'Well, we do live in the same dreary bed-sit in Chalk Farm. He's in the attic. I'm on the ground floor'

Oxley, whose mouth had dropped just perceptively, took his cue to leave. 'Please to meet you Olive. Sorry I have to leave.'

Olive, apparently, had assuaged all doubts about Thursfield's sexual tendencies. The young couple deserved to be left to themselves.

He got up and grabbed the black bowler hat that had sat beside him; he shook hands with Thursfield, smiled as he patted Olive on her delicate shoulder, and left.

Chapter 6

Vaux was enjoying the late-night bar crawl. It was the most effective tranquiliser against the horrors of returning to the Hotel Splendide. But he now recognized that he was once again feeling his age. This alcohol-powered nocturnal odyssey was the sort of unhealthy caper he used to indulge in when he was younger, as an ambitious reporter on the cusp of some scoop his editors had entrusted him to uncover for the ultimate glory and kudos for the paper he worked for—as well, of course, for himself. But those times were supercharged with ambition, his energy was inexhaustible, and he didn't need sleep—it interfered with his pursuit of the truth.

Life, he told himself, was catching up with him. This would be the very last assignment he would undertake for bloody B3. He was becoming so weary that even the bed at the Splendide seemed inviting. But so far, he hadn't made any contact. He felt alone and neglected. He decided to return to Chez Loury simply because it was his only lead. It was only a few blocks away towards the old port.

In the distance, he could hear the subdued rumblings of the late-night traffic around the harbour. The narrow streets, dimly lit by old lanterns that hung from iron brackets attached to the buildings, were deserted except for couples who seemed reluctant to go home and listless young men hawking drugs to any aimless punter who looked interested or bored. Vaux looked up at the shabby, shuttered building. Nothing had changed since his earlier reconnaissance.

But then he saw it, through a sash window on the third floor: a glimmer of light that projected upwards to a yellowed ceiling. He stood on the other side of the street and watched. There was no movement and no hint of any activity. He walked through the small cobbled front garden towards the door: withered plants in broken clay flowerpots served as sentries to the narrow entrance, painted blue many moons ago, faded and blistered by the hot sun. Vaux looked for a bell push. Suddenly, the door opened.

A tall, thin man in a long striped cotton *thobe* gave a slight bow and gestured with his arm for Vaux to enter. In the sepulchral blue-tiled foyer, the man silently gestured again towards the narrow staircase. Vaux nodded as the wizened Arab lightly brushed past him to climb the stairs and presumably to the man Craw had described as the key contact in the multinational effort to support MI6's Operation Mascara.

A light knock at the door, followed by two more in rapid succession. Then Vaux was ushered into the room with polite and silent gestures. He saw a dark, bulky figure sitting at a small desk at the far side of the room. An anglepoise lamp threw a round, bright light on to the leather surface and effectively obscured the man's face in the surrounding gloom.

'Ah, Westropp! *Shalom.* You don't know me, but I've heard a lot about you. My assistant, Mustafa, noticed you loitering in front of the house. So all is well.'

Vaux was caught off-guard. It had been a long time since anyone had addressed him by his old code name. But he felt a slight layer of protection enfold him. He had never liked to hear his real name used by the ephemeral occupants of the secret world. He stretched out his hand to confirm the identification. It was gripped tightly by a warm, rather damp fleshy fist. But before he could confirm his name, the man behind the desk declared that he was delighted to meet him.

'Finally, we have caught up,' Vaux said, in an attempt to imply that the cat-and-mouse game Vaux had been forced to play in Marseille was a bureaucrat-inspired waste of time.

Mishka Arenson ignored the remark. 'I have been instructed by your Mr. Craw to give you the outline of the mission at hand. If you are curious as to who I am or what masters I answer to, you will have to consult your colleagues in London.'

Vaux nodded agreement. Mishka leaned sideways and produced a bottle of Evian from behind the desk, a move that prompted Mustafa to rush forward with a small tray and two glasses.

'I have heard many stories about your various exploits, Westropp. You are practically a legend in our ranks.'

'Yes, well, thank you,' Vaux said modestly. 'And you are?'

'You can call me Mishka; that's all you have to know. And this is Mustafa, my assistant. He comes from a small town called Mascara, in Algeria.'

Vaux turned to acknowledge Mustafa, who had now retreated to his station by the door. Vaux's eyes swept around the room: yellowed walls with discolored blotches where damp had seeped in, tobacco-stained ceiling with broken curlicued friezes; a large, faded nineteenth-century canvas of tall ships docked in a fog-bound Vieux Port. Vaux had noted Mishka's wily insertion of the operation's code name. He settled into the upright chair that faced his host.

The man who called himself Mishka then opened a drawer. He extracted a manila folder. He took out one sheet of A4 paper and began to read from it in an accent Vaux recognized as part-Israeli, part London estuary, with the guttural overtones of Arabic. Then he handed the paper to Vaux.

'As you see, a major terrorist outrage is imminent. Their target is the brand-new mosque now being built in Algiers. They want to blow it sky-high. It's a pet project of Bouteflika, the president, who thinks it will bring prestige and fame to the capital. It will be the third biggest mosque in the world, after Mecca and Medina. There's a lot riding on it; in the Arab street, Bouteflika's popularity is waning. He's a sick man, and he's been in power for sixteen years now; not much of the country's oil riches have percolated down to the masses.'

'What terrorist group are we talking about?' asked Vaux.

'That's where you come in.'

'You've only told me their target.'

Mishka stood up and stroked the grey stubble on his chin. 'Now read the note I have given you. And we'll go from there.' Vaux quickly scanned the short document.

A rogue team of terrorists loosely affiliated with ISIS/AQIM is planning to blow up the Djamaa el Djazair mosque [now under construction] in Algiers. A great symbol of the Muslim world, it will [if completed] be the world's third biggest mosque after those in Mecca and Medina.

The small cell of terrorists are Algerian-born Arabs now domiciled and active in the south of France, mainly in Marseille.

YOUR TASK: To infiltrate the group of conspirators by whatever means possible. Intensive cyber and telephonic surveillance of the ISIS/AQIM splinter group reveals plans to recruit possible rogue subagents to help expedite their ultimate destructive goal.

GOOD LUCK!

Vaux got up, folded the sheet of paper, and put it in his hip pocket. As he approached the door, he heard Mishka call out.

'Oh, Westropp! Forgetting our tradecraft, are we?'

Vaux knew instantly what he meant. He handed the sheet of paper to Mustafa, who walked over to a portable shredder discreetly placed on top of a plastic waste bin under the windowsill.

'Sorry about that,' said Vaux. 'Didn't expect such a modern convenience to be available—'

'In such a dump, you mean.'

'Well, I wasn't going to say that.'

Mishka got up. He was shorter than Vaux had expected, and his ample gut fell over his waistband. He flipped a visiting card from his hand like a magician doing a card trick.

'I recommend this place. It's just by the harbour, not ten minutes away. I think you'll find it a little more amenable than the Splendide.'

Vaux took the card. 'You are heaven sent. Thanks so much.'

'Heaven had nothing to do with it. But anyway, mazel tov.'

Vaux wasn't surprised Mishka knew where he was staying. He'd have been surprised if he hadn't known.

* * *

Patrick Thursfield, in a dark grey linen suit recently purchased on his return to London from Austin Reed of Regent Street, a blue shirt with white collar, and a grey gold-striped Manchester University tie, sat opposite Bill Oxley in his small windowless office within the labyrinthine Thameside headquarters of MI6.

'How was Bude?'

'Lovely place, especially this time of year.'

'I'm talking about the GCHQ operation, not the resort town,' Oxley said with characteristic impatience.

'Oh yes, of course. Well, it was a ten-day crash course, as you know, and I think I'm much better at using and employing to their full potential the state-of-the-art communications technologies than I was before I took the course.' Thursfield had adroitly employed the phrase habitually used by the GCHQ staffers.

'Yes, well, you now probably know a lot more about those arcane areas than I do. I'm of the old school—typewriters, black telephones using what they now call landlines, one-time pads—'

'Actually, sir, there's an electronic equivalent of the old one-time pad. The latest Service-issued smartphones encrypt messages instantaneously and can be decrypted in plaintext with the press of a button. Of course, you have to have the right kind of cell phone, and passwords have to be memorised, not written down. Marvelous what they can do with algorithms these days.'

Oxley's eyes had glazed over. 'Yes, well, you're talking to a man who doesn't know the difference between these so-called algorithms and the logarithms we had beaten into us at Harrow. That being said, I'm sure you're adequately prepared for whatever comes your way.

'Now listen to me: from today, you've got a new boss— Craw, whom you already met. Deputy to Sir Nigel Adair, head of Department B3. As you already know, B3's a subgroup of MI6. Over the years, it's acquired a somewhat chequered history, but by and large, they're competent people.

'Recently, as you may have gathered, one of their veteran operatives has fallen, shall we say, under a very dark cloud of suspicion. It's extremely serious; betrayal at its worst—with untold victims who probably paid with their lives. So get your stuff together, go over to Gower Street now, and learn about your mission. You will report to Craw or Sir Nigel via these telephonic contraptions you are so familiar with.'

Thursfield felt a frisson of excitement. This is why he had applied to join Her Majesty's Secret Service, otherwise known as SIS, the Secret Intelligence Service. He was finally going to see some action in the field. Because of his degree in medieval and ancient history, his fear of being overlooked on the promotion ladder—up against brilliant and competitive scientists and electronic wizards—now faded. Perhaps the old boys in the top positions had more in common with his academic preferences than they ever had with the technocrats. Now he was to go into the field and employ his undoubted talents to chase down and bring to justice those who, to gain their own ends, menaced the Western world with violence and blackmail.

* * *

TOP SECRET

FROM: TARBOOSH
TO: Internal Special Inquiry re WESTROPP/V.
OPERATION CEDAR, 2010
Location: Beirut, Lebanon

> TASK: To uncover mole within UK's diplomatic/intelligence operations in Beirut following multiple leaks of intelligence re: our operations and strategies aimed at exposing terrorist plots and militia operations against national civilian and military targets; plus persistent 'outing' of Mi6 subagents, informants, and secret contacts in Lebanon and the Mideast.

ASSIGNED AGENTS: WESTROPP/V.; GREENE; MICKLETHWAIT [all of Dept. B3].

> Scenario: Op. Cedar got off to a disastrous start: Greene kidnapped by affiliate of Hezbollah militants, Micklethwait killed by rogue gunman at Dept. B3 safe house in suburbs of Beirut. Vaux zeroes in on suspected mole—the wife of the then UK AMBASSADOR to Lebanon. A Brazilian national, she apparently had a grudge against the Israelis

for the death of her young daughter in a cross-border firefight between Hezbollah and Israeli forces.

CHARGE: WESTROPP/V. held secret talks with Hezbollah leaders, who saw the quickest way to divert and sabotage the leaks inquiry was to point a finger at the ambassador's wife, whose motive could be ascribed to the alleged Israeli indifference to civilian casualties on Lebanon's southern border. WESTROPP/V. had initiated an affair with this party shortly after his arrival in Beirut. In retrospect, a shrewd and cynical move taken at the outset of OPERATION CEDAR.

CONCLUSION: It is strongly suggested by investigating officers that by implicating the ambassador's wife in the resolution of OPERATION CEDAR, WESTROPP/V. aborted and avoided a more thorough inquiry into potential double-agents operating within the British Embassy in Beirut.

114XM6B3

Chapter 7

The Bar du Port was small and dimly lit, its entrance in a narrow cobblestoned alley off the Rue de la Croix, within a few metres of the Quai de Rive. Vaux brushed aside the beaded curtain that covered the entrance and at once felt a familiarity with the place. Only a few insomniacs propped up the bar; it was getting on for 3.30 a.m. The pungent aroma of Gauloises hung heavily as wispy clouds of tobacco smoke lingered and shifted with the whiffs of air generated by a wobbly, slowly rotating, three-blade ceiling fan.

Behind the zinc bar, Vaux saw an attractive girl in her early twenties; black hair swept back in a pony tail, deep brown eyes, matelot sweater, and ballet flats. She reminded him of Audrey Hepburn as she smiled and approached him. Vaux looked around: two beefy middle-aged men sitting at a table at the back of the room; at the bar, a young man in blue jeans and white t-shirt who had been chatting up the barmaid, and at the far end, two *mecs* in the early stages of nocturnal oblivion.

'I've come to meet the boss,' Vaux said as he produced the business card Mishka had given him.

She tried out her English. 'But 'e is, 'ow you say? occupe—occupied?—monsieur.' She looked at the small gold watch on her thin wrist. 'Per'aps ten minutes?'

'Great,' said Vaux. Tired and worn out by the day's excursions, he tried to sound patient and understanding. A drink would help, he told himself, as she waited for his order.

'I'll have a whisky,' he said with a quick smile. As much as he would have liked, he was too tired to make small talk. He watched her as she stretched to reach a bottle on a high glass shelf behind her.

She was about to pour a big measure of Jim Beam into a tall glass packed to the brim with ice cubes.

'Non, non, ma'moiselle,' protested Vaux. '*Scotch* whisky, *s'il vous plait.*' She looked at the few dusty bottles on the glass shelves behind her. Again she stretched up to the top shelf to bring down a half-full bottle of Dewar's. Then she plunked down a large glass jug of water and returned to talk to the young man at the end of the bar. Vaux, who had suffered a sexual dry spell since his one-night stand with Angela Morris, watched her sashay down the bar and felt a slight stirring of his moribund libido.

A big man suddenly appeared through a heavy velvet curtain at the other end of the bar; he nodded to the two men who were still absorbed in a voluble and heavily gestured conversation with one another and approached Vaux. He suddenly stopped in his tracks—a theatrical gesture of shock.

'Stone the bloody crows, if it ain't Michael bloody Vaux, renowned international journalist, known in the newspaper business as Mr. Bloody Scoop.'

Vaux instantly recognized the apparent proprietor of the Bar du Port: Gerald Dawson, a veteran photojournalist he had met off and on over many years on international assignments. An Aussie who had never lost his Down Under accent and never changed his outback appearance: long, shaggy blond-grey hair, baggy blue jeans that slipped below his ample girth, his big feet clad in white socks and trainers. His blue penetrating eyes, now open wide in surprise, had always seemed too small for his fleshy round face.

Vaux got up from his stool and gripped Dawson's outstretched hand. 'I never expected to see *you* here,' he said.

'Blimey O'Reilly, nor did I to see you, mate. I thought you were probably dead by now. Life in the fast lane and all that. We journalists have short lives, you know. I read that somewhere recently.'

Vaux shook his head in disbelief. He raised his glass. 'Here's to a long life for both of us then.'

'Well, I never. Strewth! I can't believe it. I was asked to reserve a room but given no name. It's upstairs, number three, old sport. Ready for immediate occupancy.'

Dawson pulled out a bar stool and manoeuvred his bulky frame to sit closer to his old colleague.

Vaux said, 'So what made you come down here, Gerry? Never dreamed you would settle down to this sort of life. The south of France maybe, but a bar?'

'You must be joking. I've practically lived in bars all my life. I remember first meeting you in some seedy joint in Amsterdam. Some bloody international confab, if I remember right. All jaw-jaw and no action.'

Without asking, Dawson poured more Scotch into Vaux's glass. He got up and went round to the bar to pull a draught *pils* from a small red barrel on the counter. The two men reminisced for another hour until Dawson handed over a Yale key with a big, bold 3 written on the tag.

Vaux was too tired to examine the sheets. But the room was clean, and a small en-suite bathroom bore no traces of previous guests.

* * *

Mishka, in black turtleneck sweater and blue jeans, sat up front in the small, white Citroen C3, cursing the frugality of his Tel Aviv spymasters when selecting practical vehicles for the everyday chores of running agents and networks. He hardly had room to stretch his short muscular legs.

The TGV from Paris was always on time, and he was looking forward to meeting the Operation Mascara liaison man from MI6. Within a few minutes, he would see Mustafa, in his flowing djellaba and the white taqiyah he wore to cover his bald head, escorting an elegantly dressed Englishman down the steep steps of the Gare St. Charles to where he waited just behind the frenetic taxi pickup line.

It was midday, and the weather forecaster on the car radio had called for a high of 35 degrees centigrade. He punched the key that brought up the news channel and sighed at the thought that perhaps his expected English colleague, beguiled by the charms of Paris, had missed his train. But at last, he saw two men as they descended the steps: Mustafa struggling with a heavy leather suitcase, accompanied by a tall, slim young man in a taupe linen suit and Panama hat. While Mustafa struggled to push the suitcase in the trunk, Thursfield leaned into the open window where Mishka sat and shook his hand. Mishka's grip was deliberately limp.

'Nice to meet you,' said Thursfield. 'Heard a lot of intriguing stories.'

'Try not to repeat them,' said Mishka.

Thursfield sat back in the cramped seat behind Mishka as he looked out to the grim terraced houses and shabby shops of the main station district: an exotic mix of retailers who flogged a variety of services from sex aides and porno magazines to oranges and leeks. Nobody spoke as if some tacit agreement between the three men had ruled that Mustafa deserved silence as he manoeuvred the car into the fast-moving traffic lanes.

Mishka suddenly turned around stiffly to look straight into Thursfield's blue eyes. 'We're heading for Cassis, about a ninety-minute drive east of here. I want to spend a couple of days there to brief you on what this operation is all about and how my outfit plans to help London sort this mess out.'

Thursfield showed mild surprise. 'But Vaux, or rather Westropp—sorry about that—is right here in Marseille; or so I understand.' It was a statement to elicit more information, rather than a provocative comment of the obvious.

'Of course, he is. We're in contact with him, and everything's going according to plan. I just want to sit with you for a quiet two days or so while you get acclimatised to the scene. Then you'll dive into the deep end and get this show on the road. It shouldn't take long, to be honest. It's just a question of if and when our Mr. Vaux, or Mr. Westropp, if you wish, will take the bait.'

'Of course,' said Thursfield, who after sitting for three hours on the TGV, felt more like stretching his long legs in a walk around the famous old port. 'Anyway, it's nice to meet you face-to-face after all the briefings about you and the operation.'

Mishka grunted and lapsed into a long silence while Mustafa negotiated the heavy downtown traffic.

* * *

They took the A50 auto route, heading east. The traffic was light, and they arrived in Cassis ahead of Mishka's schedule. Mustafa pulled up at a pair of tall black iron gates, lowered his window, and leaned out to punch in an entry code. The gates swung open very slowly, and Thursfield noticed the monitoring camera that sat at the top of a tall steel poll. A wide gravel sweep, lined by tall cypress trees, took them to the porticoed front doors of an elegant, rambling two-storey villa. A young man with a trimmed black beard in white shirt and blue jeans emerged and stood waiting while Mustafa opened the trunk and hauled out Thursfield's suitcase. The young man then got in the driver's seat and drove the car away.

Mishka disappeared with a terse: 'Dinner at eight; take a siesta.'

Mustafa then silently beckoned Thursfield to follow him up a broad, winding staircase to his assigned bedroom. Mustafa placed the suitcase on a low chest of drawers, nodded towards Thursfield, and silently left the room.

Thursfield took in his new surroundings: the walls were painted a pale yellow, and there were a few French impressionist prints placed haphazardly, presumably to remind guests of their host country. He looked in vain for a bathroom. He supposed he'd have to go and look for one.

He moved towards the big window and slowly opened the white venetian blinds. The view was stunning: here was the azure blue of the Mediterranean in a tranquil bay, flanked by steep white limestone cliffs and dotted with small fishing boats and big motor yachts. The exquisite view seemed to justify the long and uneventful journey from Paris.

He took off his jacket, pulled his pants off, and jumped on the bed. Mishka's instincts had been right: he was tired, and he decided to have a nap before exploring the house for a bathroom.

But his brain wouldn't cooperate. He was excited at the prospect of some action in the field; he reassured himself that the high-tech surveillance tools duly supplied by the boffins at Vauxhall Cross would quite likely make him the key player in Operation Mascara. After all, he had been given all the latest gadgets and spyware needed to finish the mission successfully. Images of the esoteric tech tools he would be using to crack the case drifted before his closed eyes. The last one was his favourite: the latest state-of-the-art RF detector listening device, the size of Olive's red lipstick tube. He relished the thought of listening in to all of Vaux's secret and confidential cell phone conversations.

Thursfield was woken by a rapid knock at the door. He jumped up, grabbed a pair of jeans from his suitcase, and opened the door to Mustafa, still in his white djellaba, worry written all over his face.

'Mister, you expected downstairs in ten minutes, please.'

As Mustafa turned to leave, Thursfield called him back. 'I need a shower or a bath, Mustafa. Where do I go?'

Mustafa looked puzzled. Then he pointed to a door directly opposite his own room.

'Oh! Okay, down shortly.'

Chapter 8

Alan Craw checked into the five-star Hotel Le Dieux, where he had reserved a suite on the fourth floor. He had flown that morning on an Air France flight, having spent the previous night at the British embassy in Paris. He had travelled alone and considered his senior Foreign Office status justified the extravagance of the two-bedroom suite. Besides, he told himself, the probe he was heading promised to be a landmark in the annals of MI6—the ultimate exposure of a long-time traitor who had cleverly hidden his real loyalties to Britain's historic enemies.

His cell phone chimed the first notes of Andy Razaf's *I'm in the Mood for Love.*

Dawson never bothered to introduce himself: 'You want to see 'im alone, I take it.'

Craw recognized the Aussie twang. 'Yes, of course. I haven't worked out exactly what my line will be, but I don't see any harm in mentioning our connection, do you?'

'Blimey. Now you mention it, I don't really know, mate.'

Craw visibly squirmed at the strong Down Under accent in general and the word *mate* in particular. 'So what exactly is your game plan?' he asked.

'*My* game plan? Stone the crows, you're the boss. I don't have a clue. I'm just—what I think the jargon is—a "joe," and you're my handler, louse.'

Craw cringed at what he supposed was an Australian term of endearment; he particularly disliked spy jargon spoken among agents, subagents, cut-outs, or anyone else who came within the shadowy orbit of the intelligence world.

'Yes, well, I am quite confident that my overall strategy is sound. It's just a few of the tactics that have to be thought through with a very critical eye. I'd appreciate your input. You've been around our game for years, and I want you to know we regard you as a major asset in these parts—'

'Bottom line, you want my ass round there soonest.'

'Make it around eleven, please.'

'You've got it.'

Dawson put the receiver down and shook his head. 'Blimey O'Reilly, why did they send a bloody pommy like that for this caper?' He was shaking his head in disbelief when he looked up at the looming and familiar figure of Michael Vaux, his old colleague and sole guest at the small pension above the bar.

'Morning, sport. How did yer sleep?'

'Like a baby.'

'I should hope so, with all that booze. Which reminds me, I'll have to get another bottle of the Dewar's—that was my last you finished off.'

'Look,' said Vaux, 'I don't know quite whether I'll be staying another night. I have some business to do, and I'm waiting to hear from an associate on where and when I go from here.'

Dawson gave Vaux a look that suggested he may know something about his next move.

'Oh, then while you wait for your associate to contact you, just make yourself at home. I'll get the girl to rustle up something to eat. You must be starving, mate. What'll it be—a full English?'

* * *

Mishka sat alone at the head of a long rosewood dining table in the dimly lit dining room. Thursfield acknowledged him with a nod and saw that he was to be the sole guest. At the far end of the austerely laid table was the only other place setting.

Mishka, in a white shirt, sleeves rolled up over his fleshy arms, just perceptibly smiled a greeting.

'We are dining alone together, Mr. Thursfield. You will find the buffet very appetizing—cold beef, potato salad, coleslaw. Self-service. I'm sure you are very hungry after the day's travels.'

Thursfield had been looking forward to a more social evening. He wondered what had happened to Mustafa and the young man who had greeted them when they arrived. But security considerations were probably paramount.

'Yes, I am rather hungry.' Thursfield was being diplomatically polite. He was in fact famished; his last meal had been a ham sandwich in the stand-up bar of the Paris-Marseille TGV.

'Lovely view, by the way—from my room.'

'Ah, yes. The small picturesque inlet is as pretty as a jewel.'

'Framed by those magnificent white cliffs. I've never seen anything quite so striking.'

'Not even the white cliffs of Dover? They are called *calanques* in these parts—tall limestone cliffs that dot the coast and the interior of this part of Provence.'

'Oh,' replied Thursfield. 'I've seen Dover's cliffs countless times. Dover's cliffs are chalk, of course.'

Thursfield got up and headed for the long oak sideboard. The sliced beef was a bit overcooked for his taste, but the creamy coleslaw looked good, as did a large salad bowl of lettuce and tomatoes. He doused the food with a dressing that looked like a blend of olive oil and balsamic vinegar.

The two men ate in silence. Then Mishka looked up, wiped his mouth with a big starched napkin, and stared down the table at Thursfield, who was wiping his plate with a thick chunk of baguette.

'Before we get into the nitty-gritty—as you say in English—of your assignment, I think you should be aware of my role in all this. Our two services often cooperate in these days of terrorism and unending hostilities between the West and its enemies.

'As you know full well, the Cold War's over. Russia has taken a back seat in opposition to the West, and our main enemies are now centred in the Middle East and North Africa. It is no secret that the Arab world is hostile towards Israel, and because America and Britain are our staunch allies, a hostile environment imbues relations between the Arabs and the West as a whole.

'So if you ever had any doubts, take it as written that our intelligence services often act in coordination with those of America and Britain—and France, for that matter.' Mishka paused as he filled his wine glass with Vichy water.

'I believe you've already been fully briefed about Operation Mascara. The name, by the way, derives from a small town in Algeria, south of Oran, where we have an effective undercover presence ...'

'You mean Mossad, I take it.'

'Of course. Our set-up in Algeria dates back to the colonial days, when the French turned a blind eye to our activities due to the fact they viewed us as assets in the war against the Algerian independence movement. "The enemy of my enemy is my friend," as they say. In those pre-independence days, our agents also operated out of Constantine, a town in eastern Algeria not far from the Tunisian border. But since the Algerian rebels won their war with metropolitan France, we mainly work out of a town named Ghardaia, quite a ways south.

Mishka took another swig of mineral water.

'Any questions?'

'From my briefings in London, sir, I understand that Operation Mascara is a feint—'

'Yes, of course. I don't want to mislead you. It is what I like to call a sophisticated ruse—the sole purpose of which is to expose a long-time trusted MI6 operative as a traitor. The outcome should once and for all confirm our contention that the person in question is an undercover agent for the Syrian side in particular and for the so-called Arab cause in general.'

'Right,' said Thursfield.

'We call our teams here the *Metsada*—our term for the special operations officers who work for Mossad's research division. For your ears only, they now work in fifteen zones—but the Maghreb, which includes Morocco, Tunisia, and Algeria, is our major area of activity.'

Thursfield raised a finger. 'May I ask you what I hope is not an impolite question.'

'Go right ahead.' Mishka smiled benignly.

'What is the relevance of this very interesting briefing, if this whole thing is a fictional exercise to entrap our wayward spy?'

Mishka looked genuinely hurt. He shook his head and covered his eyes with his stubby hands.

'You are very young, my friend. Perhaps I assume too much when I feel the need to fill in the essential background of our project here. Perhaps I have bored you.' He looked down at the empty dinner plate before him as though making a prayer, thanking God for his nourishment.

Thursfield felt guilty. Perhaps he had shown signs of impatience and disinterest in the older man's history lesson. But the man from Mossad was a seasoned operator of one of the finest services in the world, a ruthless outfit perhaps, but an effective one. No scandals like Philby or Blunt, few fiascos, and many unsung triumphs.

Thursfield said, 'And what you call the Metsada. What is the reason we are calling them in to help in this particular exercise?'

Mishka got up, pushed his chair back, and headed for the door. He turned around to look straight at Thursfield. 'To operate effectively, you have to know all the moving parts of a critical situation. I want you to be aware that we have the full cooperation of the DRS in our Algerian operations. We work closely together, and I wouldn't want you to be ignorant of that fact.'

'The DRS?'

Mishka gave out a theatrical sigh. 'Algeria's *Departement du Renseignment et de la Securite*—in English, the Department of Intelligence and Security. In plain language, their spy agency.'

'Yes, of course,' Thursfield said, embarrassed by his ignorance.

'Look, your Mr. Craw will explain everything. I hope you have come with your bag of tricks. We have to catch this man in the act of betrayal. Unfortunately, we can only do it these days with your high-falutin' electronic gizmos and gadgets. Have a good night.'

With that, Mishka swept out of the room, leaving the double doors slightly open.

Thursfield was now alone. He saw that the dining table was surrounded by eight upright chairs and wondered if they were ever occupied in one sitting.

He glanced around the room for a drinks trolley, but the long oak sideboard only offered several more bottles of mineral water. After about five minutes, he skipped up the winding staircase, two steps at a time. When he got to his room, he was surprised to see that he had left the door ajar. Or had he? He pushed the door open and reached for the light switch. Someone had rifled through his open suitcase: socks on the floor, underpants scattered, and his trainers thrown against the white wood paneling beneath the windows. But his electronic box of tricks [mainly encrypted phones, RF detectors, GPS equipment and microscopic listening devices] concealed in the false bottom of the conventional Delsey suitcase remained undiscovered and untouched.

Chapter 9

Gerald Dawson had lived in Marseille for seven years. He was fifty-five when he decided to give up his career as a wandering photojournalist for the sake of a young girl he had met while on assignment for *Travel & Leisure.* Her name was Peigi, and her father was the grandson of a Vietnamese lawyer who had worked for the French colonial administration in Saigon. He had fled to France along with the defeated colonial government, in the wake of the Communist takeover of 1955.

Peigi was beautiful: the slight physique, the long jet black hair, skin the color of dark amber. To Dawson, she was *the* most beautiful girl in the world. He was damned if he'd risk losing her just because his peripatetic job demanded long absences from home base. It did not boost his confidence to know that he was old enough to be her father and that younger, no doubt more virile men were hovering in the background, eager to wrest her from a middle-aged, over-the-hill Aussie.

Dawson's fluctuating annual income was the price he paid for his freedom from the sort of office politics and internal intrigues he knew his colleagues of the press had to cope with on an everyday basis. So when, late in the evening, a rather diffident and grey man approached him at the bar of the Club de la Presse, he was all ears. He was open to any deal that would boost his war chest, and a vast worldly experience told him that the rather corpulent, balding man in the grey business suit may well have something to offer that was worth considering.

To cut a long story to the bare bones, as Dawson told his closest allies, the man from London had offered to finance the purchase of a property that would serve as a refuge for the odd out-of-town visitor who would from time to time be guided his way. All aboveboard and official, said the man, having taken details of Dawson's bank account numbers, current address, and so on. The safe house, as the man called it, would not be available for his own use. He was to act as a sort of concierge, you see, arranging for cleaners and some basic food and drinks in the refrigerator. In return for receiving the purchase price for such a property, whose ownership would be in his name, he would reveal to no one the details of the deal—for pain of violating the Official Secrets Act of Her Britannic Majesty's government. Understood? Dawson understood.

He never took what he called the London connection very seriously. His world travels had inured him to the clandestine dealings of national governments, and London had—despite the dribbling away of the empire—been no exception. The man had called himself Arthur, and on consummation of the deal, he bestowed on Dawson the code name Outback.

Dawson's life had at last established some permanency. He borrowed money on the security of the property that had fallen into his lap, thanks to the generosity of his London employers. Giving him full ownership title was as an assurance against the discovery by zealous French bureaucrats of a British-orchestrated deal that threatened internal security and sovereignty.

He used this money as a deposit for a rundown café called the Bar du Port. He did the place up, helped by a small army of local *mecs*, all of whom seemed to have had wide experience in the art of renovations and general window-dressing.

Dawson had never been happier. But then came the deluge. One year after acquiring Le Bar du Port, Peigi was run down by a taxi one foggy evening as she was crossing the busy Quai de Rive on an errand to buy a bag of croissants for the next day's breakfast. She died two hours later in the emergency ward at the European Hospital on the Rue Desiree.

Dawson was devastated. He got drunk, went to bed with several bottles of vodka, and stayed there for five days.

The months went by, and a few years too. Time helped heal the pain of his loss. And meanwhile, he had to attend to his bar as well as oversee the safe house on the appropriately named Rue de Refuge, where the occasional shadowy guest was cared for but largely left alone. Dawson kept his distance—apart from the necessary housekeeping such an arrangement made necessary. Then a few weeks ago, the call came through on his encrypted cell phone. His services would be required in the very near future. A Mr. Alan Craw would be calling him regarding a new guest for the safe house on the Rue de Refuge.

* * *

Craw stood by the tall casement windows that look out to Le Panier, a bohemian, somewhat neglected district of Marseille that had failed to benefit from the city's gentrification and rehab drive of the early 2000s. This was the Arab quarter, or at least where the refugees and wanderers from the Maghreb congregated in shabby, narrow streets with pavements that suddenly turned into steep flights of steps and wandered off to even narrower cobbled alleyways canopied by overhanging wires and thick cables. The stucco walls of the buildings, covered in colorful and grotesque graffiti and bright street art, seemed to lean towards inevitable collapse.

Craw gazed down at the milling crowds as they went about their daily errands and chores. Shouts, whistles, screams, the clang of bicycle bells, blaring car horns, the high-pitched whine of motor scooters—the familiar din of the Arab street. Craw's lips curled just perceptibly with Anglo-Saxon distaste. He pulled the rusting metal shutters together to lessen the glare and mute the raucous street noises. Then he heard the thumps of someone mounting the narrow wooden staircase to the second floor and chose to sit down on a shabby leather armchair that faced the door. A bunch of metal keys rattled, a key was inserted, and the heavy bulk of Gerry Dawson stood before him.

Dawson took a theatrical backward step in mock surprise at seeing a strange man facing him in what was supposed to be a secure safe house. He had spoken to Craw on the phone more times than he cared to remember, but he had never met the man face to face.

He uttered the inevitable and appropriate phrase: 'Mr. Craw, I presume.'

Craw, his eyes glued to Dawson's wide-brimmed kangaroo bush hat, stood up. The two men shook hands. Dawson quickly walked into the small kitchen. He opened the door of a mini-bar that stood on the white-tiled countertop and produced two bottles of Kronenbourg 1664. He flipped the caps off and walked through to where Craw was still standing

'Oh, not for me, old boy. Still trying to digest my breakfast. I won't stay long. Just wanted to connect with you to make sure you are fully briefed on this rather delicate operation.'

'Operation Mascara, you mean?' Dawson's gravelly voice seemed to reverberate through the small flat. He pulled an upright chair away from the small plastic-covered table by the kitchen door.

Craw cringed at the breach of security—and, as he saw it, a breach of decorum. Even the clandestine world in which the two men operated surely possessed some basic rules of professional etiquette. So he produced a loud, nervous cough, as if its resonance could in some way muffle Dawson's outrageously loose talk. Dawson looked wide-eyed at Craw as the fastidious Englishman quickly put his index finger to his lips to command silence.

'Come on, mate, I know the place is bugged, but the listeners are our people, eh?'

Craw gave up any attempt to persuade the Australian of the need for more discretion.

'I came here just a few days ago via Paris. I don't know whether you have been briefed fully by a contact, code name Mishka—'

'No, mate. I know nothing. This fellow Mishka called me on behalf of the—well, you know, your people, and asked me to put up a gentleman who needed a place to sleep for a few nights. Well, I did, didn't I? We let out two of our rooms if we can—'

'Yes, yes. All right. Well, let's leave it like that.'

'Well, you could have blown me down when the man who came round that night from this fellow Mishka's place, was a former colleague of mine that I've known for donkey's years—on and off, of course. Would you believe it? Used to bump into him on all sorts of assignments.'

Craw sat stone-faced, determined not to reveal any surprise. 'Yes, well, just remember that his code name is Westropp—Derek Westropp. That's his name as long as he's involved in this operation. Do you understand?'

'Right, mate. I'll make every effort to remember that.'

Craw muttered, 'You must try. And may I remind you of *your* code name—Outback.'

Dawson grunted.

Craw let the matter drop. 'My mission is to make sure everything goes according to plan. You don't need to contact me. I shall be monitoring the operation on a daily basis. Mishka is our main source of information, a key man whose organisation has furnished us with the facts we need to bring Westropp in. You do understand, don't you?'

'Not really. I think I'm missing something. But I really don't want to know. My job's to keep this place functioning. That's the deal, right, old sport?'

'Yes, well, if you have any questions, please address them to me. Meanwhile, a man called Thursfield will be here in an hour to re-jig the listening devices and check on the cameras. So would you stay here until he arrives with his box of tricks?'

'Sure, that's what I'm paid for.'

'And please remember to use your code name in all communications until Operation Mascara is concluded.'

'Of course, mate—Outback. Not easy for a bloke from Down Under to forget.'

'Good show, old bean. Bye for now.'

Craw hadn't used that archaic expression in years. He supposed that for some reason Dawson reminded him of a character in some 1960s adventure movie. Something to do with crocodiles. He was happy to leave him to his own devices. Now he would retreat to the comfortable confines of his hotel. As he closed the door, he saw that Dawson was still wearing his absurd hat.

Chapter 10

Gerald Dawson returned to the Bar du Port in mid-afternoon. He was not surprised to see Vaux sitting alone at the zinc bar, a bottle of beer in front of him as he scanned the *New York Times International*.

'Hey louse, got some news for yer.'

Vaux looked up. He smiled and sipped his Heineken. 'What's that, then?'

'I've been asked to take you to your new abode, mate. Can't stay here forever. I can't afford it.'

'Afford it? What are you talking about, Gerry? Give me the bill, and I'll pay my way. You know that. But I suppose you need the room.'

'No, no. You can stay forever and a fortnight, as far as I'm concerned, mate. Crikey, how shall I put it? Look, does the name Westropp mean anything to you? Derek Westropp?'

Vaux's thoughts went swirling around all the possibilities. Had there been a leak at the highest level of Department B3?

Or, God forbid, through the reputed sieve of the Vauxhall Cross bureaucracy?

Then a less panicky explanation occurred to him: he had been guided by a series of murky manoeuvres to this odd one-name character they called Mishka, who in turn had sent him to the Bar du Port, where he had been shocked to meet an old hack he assumed had died years ago. But now it seemed that Dawson was probably a joe, doing the odd top-secret errand for MI6 under a cast-iron cover.

Vaux drained his glass, placed it on the bar, and turned to Dawson. 'Yes, I've come across Westropp in my travels. I think he used to work for the *Evening Standard*—sort of a roving correspondent.' Vaux recalled Operation Helvetia, his first spy mission, when he posed as a Mr. Derek Westropp, a reporter for that venerable London paper, covering a big international confab in Geneva. The code name stuck.

'Well, fair dunkum. That explains it, then.'

'Explains what?'

Dawson then lightly thumped Vaux between the shoulders. 'Come on, sport—we're working together again. Like old times, only we don't have to answer to any of those snarky night editors and rewrite men, eh?'

Vaux realised his cover story had misfired. Two and two *did* make four, so he might as well give in. 'Okay, Gerry, you win. But this character Mishka, who sent me here. Where does he fit in?'

Dawson looked around the bar and across his shoulder. There were only three other customers sitting at the far end of the saloon. At a table at the narrow entrance to the toilets, a young man sat chatting up Dominique, the bar girl with the pony tail; Vaux had met her the previous evening.

'Now that's a question that I cannot answer, mate. Need-to-know and all that. They treat me like a bloody mushroom—keep me in the dark and feed me shit.

'All I know is that he's new on the scene. Some connection with Mossad. They're pretty heavy down here. Marseille's a sort of branch office to Mossad's operations in Paris. They say Paris is an Israeli playground these days. The French don't like it, but they can't do much; the Israelis use the diplomatic card and go running to the Elysee bloody Palace as soon as the French intelligence boys sniff out some sort of conspiracy.

'They say they planned the assassination of one of Hamas's top big wigs in Dubai recently, all from some hotel room in the Paris suburbs. That was a very sophisticated operation, mate; they found computers, secure phones, the whole works. All this of course, right under the nose of the DGSE.' [Note 4]

Vaux said, 'He has a sort of sidekick, an Arab named Mustafa. Have you ever met him?'

'Nah, probably his bum boy, if you ask me.'

They agreed to meet up later that afternoon after Dawson's obligatory siesta and Vaux's expedition to buy a few books; he envisioned lots of idle, waiting-around time in the days ahead.

* * *

Mishka Arenson, known universally among friends and enemies alike as Mishka, was Mossad's point man in the south of France. He was in his early fifties, with thick grey hair and always on a diet to offset his middle-aged spread. His duties took him to many European countries, but rumour had it that he had two homes—a modest apartment in the earthy Eighteenth Arrondissement overlooking the Basilica de Sacre Coeur, and a beach house in Tel Aviv. He often said he preferred running operations out of Marseille, where clandestine activities would often be facilitated by the active Jewish community in the port city.

Mishka never adopted an official title and had the habit of disappearing for months and then suddenly reappearing to tackle a sudden crisis or perhaps orchestrate a tactical manoeuvre to strike at and, where possible, reverse a perceived victory won by his adversaries—usually a Hamas sleeper cell bent on a violent reminder to the French government of the need for even-handedness when it came to the eternal Israeli-Arab conflict.

Mishka silently mounted the stairs to the apartment on the Rue de Refuge. He put his ear to the glossy black door and heard movements from inside and the low hum of a transistor radio. He even recognised the tune: a current French hit by Nicky Jam, aka Nick Rivera, an American pop singer more famous in France than in his native country. He recalled the agreed-upon knocking sequence: two sharp knocks in quick succession, followed by three spaced, gentler ones.

Thursfield opened the door. Both men shook hands and Thursfield wondered whether Mishka had just arrived from his villa in Cassis.

'My boss told me to expect you,' said Thursfield as he knelt to finish the emplacement of a listening device under the wide rim of a white, earth-filled ceramic pot in the far corner of the room. The pot nurtured a small, withered miniature palm tree.

Mishka grunted. He was wearing a white, short-sleeved shirt, baggy blue jeans, and well-worn trainers. He looked around the room, and the first thing that struck him was the general tidiness. The place looked unlived-in, as if awaiting a new occupant. He went through to the kitchen and saw none of the domestic detritus he expected. He inspected the mini-bar and wasn't surprised to see it stacked with more beer cans than snack food. On the counter-top, a steel electric stove with two burners; then on a shelf above the cooker, he saw a bottle of whisky with a yellow label and assumed the boys had bought it for the new occupant.

He went back to the living room. 'Where is the man expected to sleep?' he asked Thursfield.

'The couch folds down,' Thursfield said as he pointed to the long, low chesterfield at right angles to the casement windows.

'The place is a bit small, no?' Mishka asked softly.

'I suppose they didn't want to pay a high rent,' Thursfield said in defense of his employers. He was putting the finishing touches to the installation of a combined micro-camera and a UHF Wi-Fi transmitter under the top frame of the small fifties-style television cabinet.

Mishka went through to the kitchen again. He found a bottle of Evian at the bottom of the fridge and took several swigs.

Then he heard two sharp knocks followed by three gentler taps in quick succession.

Thursfield went to open the door. He had never met Vaux in person, only seen pictures of him in various surroundings, taken surreptitiously at different times of his employment with Department B3. He certainly hadn't changed much, he thought. He recalled the right code name. 'Mr. Westropp! Pleased to meet you.'

Thursfield looked quickly around the room to make sure he had left no telltale signs of his handiwork. Vaux grasped his hand and then approached Mishka, who had been hovering in the background.

Mishka wanted Thursfield to disappear. 'Are we done?'

Then, as if to answer any suspicious question Vaux could be harbouring, he declared, 'We were just recalling old times. Thursfield's been with us on several operations, and I hadn't seen him for a couple of years.'

Thursfield understood. 'Yes. I must be off. Nice to have met you again. Now I must be getting along.' He picked up a big leather bag that looked like a lawyer's briefing case, shook hands with both men, and rattled down the stairs.

'We agree that you are here for the briefing,' said Mishka.

Vaux thought it was a rather odd statement but affirmed that was why he had come.

'Meanwhile, I take it you are moving in here. According to your Mr. Craw, that is.'

'Indeed, yes.'

'At any rate, this won't take long.'

On the third floor of the terraced house on the Rue de Refuge, Thursfield had set up an operations room; it housed all the necessary electronic equipment he needed to monitor Vaux's activities and any conversations with co-conspirators. As he understood it from his briefings with Craw, Vaux—aka Westropp—was very likely within a matter of days to get into contact with, or communicate with, or possibly have a physical one-on-one parley with some Arab terrorists.

After leaving Vaux with Mishka, he loudly descended the one flight of uncarpeted wooden stairs to street level, only to turn around in an instant and quietly tiptoe up two steps at a time, three flights to his operations room. He took off his suit jacket and tossed it on top of an ancient and decrepit chest of drawers. Then he fell into a high-backed leather swivel chair, amid his beloved monitoring equipment, earphones at the ready to listen to any incoming or outgoing phone calls on the archaic landline. Vaux's MI6-issued smartphone would already have been conveniently compromised, and he would deal with that hook-up later. On the desk in front of him stood a small, boxy device that housed a minute speaker. He flipped a switch and heard Mishka's husky but distinct voice as Vaux/Westropp received his briefing.

Chapter 11

Ten days after Vaux moved in to the cramped second-floor apartment on the Rue de Refuge in the bustling Panier district of Marseille, he reminded himself once again of that old Secret Service shibboleth: "Espionage is a waiting game." They taught him that at the Portsmouth training school where, a decade ago, he had taken a fourteen-day crash course designed especially for undercover agents who were recruited for the occasional operation—talented and promising, in Craw's words, but hardly of long-term career material.

He lay on the fold-down bed, arms clasped behind his head, stark naked against the 95 degree heat. The ancient, rattling air conditioner installed in one of the casement windows had given up its strenuous efforts to blast cool air into the hot and humid room, and a replacement had been promised.

His thought processes were slowed by the enervating heat, but he tried hard to assess the situation he was now in. Should he be more active—and if so, what to do? Go out into the Arab quarter, strike up friendships, and maybe meet some street kids who always knew a neighborhood's secrets and characters, perhaps even storied Arab fighters, better than any alien outsider.

But Craw's instructions had dissuaded him from any immediate action. Craw had said that he was working in cooperation with the DGSE, and before long he, Vaux, would be contacted by a mole within the terrorist cell who would be able to guide him in a joint Anglo-French effort to expose the conspiracy to blow up the Djamaa el Djazair mosque and arrest the culprits. Characteristically, Craw had omitted to mention what Vaux had perceived as the key player in the operation—Mossad. But he did, as was his wont, warn that time was of the essence, even though Vaux had detected little urgency in the days since he had holed up here in these dingy, claustrophobic digs.

It was too hot even to read, always a good time-killer for Vaux, who had bought several paperbacks by E.M. Forster to help him dream of the golden years of the early twentieth century, when the grandparents he never knew had enjoyed that peaceful Edwardian era, when no cold war existed and terrorism was confined to a few fanatic religious sects out of the Indian subcontinent.

He was suddenly jolted by the jangle of his cell phone which lay within reach on the bed. 'Hello?'

'Oh, blimey! You're still alive and kicking, then. It's your old mate Gerry. Where the 'ell 'ave you been all this time?'

'Remember the place you told me about in the Panier district?'

'Yeah. You met that tosser Craw there.'

'That's where I'm holed up. Thought you knew that.'

'Nah, mate. No one tells old Gerry anything. Why don't you pop round for a drink? Any time.'

'I'm sort of on stand-by, Gerry. I'll call you when I get a break.'

'Okay, mate. Stay safe.'

Upstairs, on the third floor, Thursfield's electronic alarm signaled an incoming phone call. He tuned into his treasured RF detector that should have located the cell phone number and location. But the screen was blank. He adjusted his earphones but heard a constant buzz, as if someone was jamming the circuits.

* * *

Vaux, now sweating profusely, had just managed to finish chapter 2 of *Howard's End* when he heard a gentle knock at the door. Despite the enervating heat, he jumped up and slid into his jeans in the happy anticipation of some human company.

Before him stood petite, pony-tailed Dominique, the girl behind the bar at the Bar du Port. Defying the heat, she looked fresh and younger than when he had last seen her—but that was probably because of the coarse and dank environment of the bar where she worked.

They stood looking at each other for some time before Vaux pulled himself out of shock and welcomed her over the threshold. She wore tight blue jeans, and a yellow halter covered perky, small breasts. The deep red of her lipstick exaggerated her full lips.

'Bonjour, Monsieur Westropp,' she said in a girlish, laughing way, as if they had just met by coincidence.

'Bonsoir, ma'moiselle,' replied Vaux.

Upstairs, Thursfield's recording machine flipped on, and he quickly turned off the small television set he had installed to help alleviate the boredom of his twenty-four-hour monitoring duties. He wrapped the earphones around his head, and his eyes widened as he listened to the subdued female voice conversing with Vaux's low, hard-to-detect drawl.

Dominique lost no time with formalities. She stepped out of her white ballet flats, whipped off her halter top, and wriggled out of her jeans.

'*Il est trop chaud, non?*' she said, protesting the heat.

Vaux knew he didn't have to say very much. And he guessed he owed one to his old newspaper colleague.

Upstairs on the third floor, Thursfield struggled to get the three concealed cameras operative so he could see what was going on. But none of the cameras focused directly on the fold-out bed—a serious oversight, as Craw commented at a later briefing. So all he could do was to listen wistfully to the moans and groans of two people making languid love—and the occasional angled glimpse of a long, tanned slender leg and a pale male ankle.

* * *

Some twenty-six kilometres east of the torrid safe house on the Rue de Refuge, Mishka Arenson sat alone in the cool, long oak-paneled dining room at his bolt hole overlooking the picturesque bay of Cassis. He had become impatient at the slow progress of Operation Mascara and felt an urgent need to get the whole enterprise wrapped up so he could pursue more productive endeavours.

Michael Vaux had been a thorn in his flesh for over a decade—ever since his suspected seduction by the Syrian intelligence services and probable conversion to the general Arab cause. He had heard that Vaux relented, that he claimed to have been seduced by drugs and a pretty Syrian agent, a Palestinian by birth, to mislead his MI6 masters about the secretive Syrian-Russian arms deal that Vaux had falsely claimed to be significantly smaller than Israel and its US ally had feared.

Mishka had spent many hours in Mossad's archival records department in Tel Aviv, where he had closely studied Department B3 operations subsequent to Operation Helvetia, in which Vaux had played major roles. He was agreeably surprised when he found further facts that would seem, to any sceptical but fair-minded eye, to incriminate the MI6 operative in surreptitiously aiding and abetting the traditional enemies of the state of Israel.

As a result of his assiduous and lonely research efforts, Mishka, with the strong approval of Mossad's chief of security, had sent a series of memos to Vauxhall Cross. It took three years or so to extract any response, but finally, the anonymous mandarins at

MI6's Thameside headquarters conceded that he might have a case, so they at last decided to put his suspicions to the test. So be it. He wanted to end the water-treading and get on with it.

In any case, he was totally convinced that the ultimate goal of the Arab world was, at worst, the destruction of Israel or, at best, the continuation of unacceptable pressures on Israel to get out of conquered Arab lands—in particular the West Bank and the Golan Heights [Note 5].

He knew that such goals were totally rejected by the majority of the Israeli people, and he was happy to serve his country—an island of democracy in the Middle East—for as long as he drew breath. But his patience with the current operation was growing thin. The Brits had cooperated, and MI6 indicated that they agreed with his overall objective of finally calling their renegade agent to account. But the Limeys were experts at foot-dragging, and it was time to take action and finally resolve the issue.

Everything was now in place: Vaux, aka Westropp, had been cornered, and all that was needed was the fiction of an Algerian terrorist spilling the beans to this British traitor, who would presumably then make contact with the Arab side to warn them that unless they took evasive action, they were sitting ducks.

Massive raids and a roundup of any suspect Arab nationalist/ terrorist cells would be inevitable and in consequence would represent a colossal setback to the Arab cause in France. Vaux, of course, would be caught red-handed as he tried to make contact with the enemy. That, at any rate, was the overall strategy.

Now he waited patiently for the arrival of Mustafa, who had been asked to bring in some chocolate banka cakes, Mishka's favourite mid-morning snack. He heard the gentle movements of his long-serving Tunisian factotum as he made his tentative way to the dining room from the entrance hall. The two men nodded to each other. Mustafa put down the plate of banka cakes and filled Mishka's wine glass with fizzy Evian water.

'Mustafa, it is time to act. I want you to contact your Algerian friend and give him the go-ahead. The operation is about to begin. Can you tell him to get into action as soon as possible? He knows the drill, and we are getting impatient.'

'Yes, sir. I saw him last evening, and he is ready to act on my say-so.'

Mishka grasped Mustafa's hand and wrapped it with both his hands as a warm gesture of friendship and loyalty.

The two men had met when Mishka was a young, ambitious intelligence officer in the Israeli Defense Forces. He was tasting the first delights of a hot war between Israel and its ancient Arab enemies. It was called the Yom Kippur War because it started on that sacred October day in 1973, when Egypt and Syria forces attempted to win back land both nations had lost in the Six-Day War of 1967. Mishka had just celebrated his twentieth birthday. The Yom Kippur War was a short war but victorious for Israel [Note 6].

One day, in the tranquil aftermath of the conflict, Mishka, as the day's duty officer, was quietly patrolling his company's precincts in the conquered Golan Heights, when a young Arab about his own age offered to lead him to a stash of rifles and ammunition that the Syrian army had concealed in a nearby warehouse.

The youth was named Mustafa. It was their first encounter, and Mishka soon learned about the Arab talent for dogged tenacity. So instead of shaking him off, he decided to use him. Over several months, Mustafa gained Mishka's complete confidence. Later, as Mishka graduated from the IDF to the hallowed heights of the intelligence service, the spymasters in Tel Aviv trusted and accepted Mishka's judgement of the young man's loyalties and abilities.

So Mustafa became his interpreter, his general factotum, his bodyguard, his go-between, and finally his spy for the years and decades that followed, an era that promised an eternal conflict with Israel's Arab neighbors, punctuated by cold and hot wars alike.

He had known him now for forty years, and he had been paid munificently as an informer who operated quietly out of the Arab *souk*. The steady flow of monetary rewards for Mustafa's efforts helped keep Fatima, his home-loving wife, happy and, perhaps just as important, allowed a little surplus to pay for his moderate addiction to hashish.

Chapter 12

Vaux had been cooling his heels for six days. The interlude with Dominique had been a pleasurable diversion, but he was not interested in repeating it. He had read the three Forster novels and was now about to plunge into the *quartier* to conduct a reconnaissance of likely places where the men of the neighborhood gather and sip mint tea or suck on their hookah pipes as they indulge in deep meditations about the way of the world. Now was the time to put to the test Craw's vague promise that sooner or later, someone would get in touch with him, an insider, a member of the terrorist cell Craw had turned, and who now worked for the home team, namely Department B3.

Before long, he found *La Cigale*, a small cramped café that perfectly fit the bill. Here the district's old-timers deliberated over their next strategic manoeuvre in that morning's chess game; others quietly studied their rival as he moved his pieces on the backgammon board. Several quietly scanned the *Journal La Marseillaise* for any news that could touch on their own lives. But neither the raging war in Syria nor the ongoing mass exodus of refugees from the Arab nations to Europe seemed to be of much concern to these inured men from the Maghreb.

Despite Craw's assurances that contact would soon be made, Vaux felt instinctively that only by showing himself, exposing his friendly availability, would he ever make contact with the elusive informer who had promised to expose the conspiracy to destroy the half-finished Djamaa el Djaziar mosque in Algiers.

He sat in the corner of the busy café, about fifty metres from the safe house on the Rue de Refuge. He ordered a café crème and picked up a discarded copy of the *Nice Matin* as he went over to the small table. He held the broadsheet at arm's length as he surreptitiously surveyed the clientele. He vaguely recognized a tall, thin man in a long white thobe as he shuffled in his leather babouches to the counter and ordered a glass of mint tea. The thin man sank down in the chair opposite him. Both men acknowledged each other with a nod as Vaux raised his newspaper to eye level so he could continue his surveillance unobserved.

Suddenly, Vaux saw a packet of Nassim cigarettes hovering over the top of the page. He put down the paper, smiled, and took out one of the strong Algerian cigarettes Mustafa had thrust towards him.

* * *

Sir Nigel Adair, head of Department B3, the specialist, free-wheeling group that handled projects and problems that MI6's Mideast and North African desk preferred to ignore, sat at his cluttered desk at the offices of Acme Global Consultants Ltd. on Gower Street, a comfortable distance from what Sir Nigel called 'the madhouse on the Thames.' Of course, he was well aware that he was a wholly-owned subsidiary of MI6, whose headquarters were moved several years earlier to Vauxhall Cross, the conspicuous and, according to most architectural critics, grotesque high-security building on the south bank of the river.

The ongoing probe into the loyalty of one of his seasoned operatives had irked him, and he viewed the accusations against Vaux as probably without foundation. He had read the incriminating memos from the source Tarboosh, but nobody at Vauxhall Cross had bothered to inform him of the accuser's real identity. The author of these serious indictments against one of his most effective agents remained anonymous. But in his view, the old axiom need-to-know simply did not apply. As the suspect's handler, as his spymaster, he *did* need to know.

So Sir Nigel was not in the best of moods when Alan Craw, his deputy, just back from a quick visit to Marseille, quietly entered his office, bearing a small plastic tray on which stood two Styrofoam cups of Nescafe. There were several small plastic tubs of non-dairy creamer, along with two Peak Frean chocolate digestive biscuits that had been placed on a chipped saucer.

Sir Nigel watched patiently as Craw placed the tray between them before he sat down on the ancient Windsor chair to face his boss.

'Thank you,' said Sir Nigel.

'You are welcome, sir.' Craw opened a manila folder and scanned the words that had been typed on a sheet of A4 paper. He remained silent, his usual mark of respect for his boss.

'What have you got there?' asked Sir Nigel.

'Well, sir, it's the latest brief summary from our telecommunications man, Thursfield.'

'I thought he was under Bill Oxley's jurisdiction over at Vauxhall.'

'Well, sir, yes, that is correct, strictly speaking. Oxley is the spy catcher, *par excellence*. But Thursfield is now one of his acolytes, as it were, and I have struck up quite a close, non-official sort of friendship with him. As a result, he gives me a steady flow of off-the-record reports stemming from what he is learning down there in Marseille on a day-by-day basis.'

Sir Nigel's patience was wearing thin. 'Well, get on with it, man. What do we know?'

Craw sighed, a signal to his boss not to get too excited. 'Progress is slow but sure, sir. Thursfield has set up a very efficient and esoteric operations room, of course. All conversations our Mr. Vaux may have on his mobile phone are monitored, as are any talks he has with people he may invite to the safe flat. Anywhere he decides to go is traced through the mobile phone we gave him, thanks to the wonders of GPS and Wi-Fi.'

Craw paused to let his boss take in the technical jargon he had picked up from pre-mission conversations with Thursfield. But Sir Nigel looked vague and rather bored.

Craw continued, 'Thursfield's monitoring unit is just a floor above where Vaux lives, so we don't think we will miss very much. Also, I understand from my sources that Vaux has now made contact with one of Mishka's men, and that should start the ball rolling. He will be followed twenty-four hours a day, and as I indicated, any conversations or messages, whether personal or professional, will be monitored day in, day out.'

Craw looked satisfied with his summary of the situation.

Sir Nigel's response was a sceptical grunt.

Craw waited in vain for some appropriate comment and gently pulled up his shirt cuff to glance at his gold Cartier watch—a signal that he had an important lunch date.

'You mentioned a chap named Mishka. Never heard of him. Where does he fit in?'

'He's our liaison man with Mossad's Classification Department, sir. At least, that's what Oxley tells me.'

'Classification Department? What do they do?'

'I understand, sir, that it's their job to decide whether to spy on a subject or recruit him as an agent. Sometimes, according to Mishka, they may decide to kill him.'

'Ruthless bloody bunch. Anyway, so you're telling me that Mossad are in on this mission too.'

'Yes, sir. If you ask me, it was Tel Aviv that initiated the whole business.'

Sir Nigel pushed himself up from his high-backed chair and moved slowly to the dusty sash windows that overlooked the inner well of the building. He observed the milling, talkative crowd in the accountants' office opposite. They were enjoying their innocent morning coffee break. Everyone seemed boisterously happy and oblivious to the machinations of his secret world—the treachery, the suspicions, the life-and-death questions that had to be resolved.

Chapter 13

Mustafa, after introducing himself in halting English, came quickly to the point. He mentioned he had a friend who went by the nickname of Outback. And said friend was desirous of meeting Mr. Westropp at his earliest convenience. He had some important message for him which he could not discuss on any phone.

For some reason, perhaps auto-suggestion, Vaux felt in his jacket's side pocket for his trusty grey Apple i-Phone 6s. He had bought several of these untraceable burners as soon as he had agreed to play a role in Operation Mascara. He suspected that the glossy BlackBerry issued by Technical Services had been compromised and that somewhere, some cyber thief would be reading his texts, tracking his every movement, and listening to his verbal conversations. Which was one reason his associate Thursfield could not understand why he had picked up so few of Vaux's phone calls since he set up the elaborate, audio-video surveillance systems designed by GCHQ's electronic geniuses.

Vaux tried to recall whether he had seen Mustafa's lean, stubbly face before. He decided it was of no consequence, so he got up and left the *Nice Matin* on the counter as he walked out of the La Cigale. Mustafa chose to walk a pace or two behind him, and as he looked back to him, Mustafa nodded and pointed ahead of him as if he was guiding from behind. Vaux knew the way to Le Bar du Port, so he walked with some determination towards the old port.

Suddenly, he heard a screech of brakes, then a scuffle behind him, and he was being manhandled into the back of a shiny, black Citroen C6.

Mustafa was nowhere to be seen. Vaux was shoved into the back seat, followed by his hefty bearded assailant, who quickly pulled a nylon hood over his head. He was told to stay quiet, please, and all would be well.

* * *

'This is D-Day,' mumbled Bill Oxley, chief of Vauxhall's counter-espionage division, as the tentative first steps got under way to incriminate Vaux and vaporise the persistent cloud of suspicion that hung over this legendary asset of Department B3.

Oxley was indulging in one of his peculiar habits: talking to himself. He stretched over his desk for his ultra-secure BlackBerry and punched in the code number for Marseille. But there was no answer. He looked at his black Garmin Tactix army watch and saw that it was exactly the prearranged time of day to call Craw. Oxley was puzzled, and he started to fear the worst. Had Craw disappeared in the line of duty? Anything could happen in those dank and dark back streets of Marseille.

Then the silenced phone started to give a little jig. Oxley picked it up from the desk and slid the screen button to the right.

'Yes?' he said in a strange voice.

'Oxley? It's Craw.'

'Where the hell are you? I just called Marseille.'

'Oh, I've been back a few days. Left Operation Mascara in the capable hands of my devoted agents.'

'Is that wise? I thought you said we go into action today. Westropp was to be brought in, or should I say briefed, so he can inform his Arab allies what's afoot.'

'That's precisely why I'm calling. He's been apprehended—if that's the right word—and he's now on his way, according to the latest report from Mishka, to the salubrious confines of the villa at Cassis. There he will be briefed on Operation Mascara, then released like a carrier pigeon to spread the news to the terrorists. As soon as he makes contact he'll be dead meat.'

'Figuratively speaking, of course.'

'There's a shoot-out in that city practically every day; who knows?'

'Very well, but with you here in London, who's the designated liaison man?'

'Thursfield, of course. He's perfectly capable. He's our eyes and ears. You should know; you sent him on that GCHQ training course at Bude.'

* * *

It was a mercifully short journey. After about forty minutes' drive, Vaux felt the car swerve into a gravelly driveway, swing round, and stop abruptly. He waited in vain for the hood to be pulled off his head. He heard loud voices, shouted commands in French and Arabic, his armed traveling companion gruffly responding to several men who were giving him excited directions or commands. Then the driver, who had been silent during the entire abduction operation, offered his own long-winded assessment of the situation. Suddenly, Vaux found himself being pulled out of the car by a noisy welcome committee. He was led up a few flights of steps and into a small lobby, then down three short flights of a stone staircase. His hood was removed, and he saw four men around him, one of which was the driver of the Citroen 6X. He was pushed into a small six-by-ten-foot room with no window and a small aluminium wash basin in one corner. Beside the basin stood an empty bucket that contained an unused toilet roll. Vaux thought the décor particularly ominous.

'You wait, not long,' said the chauffeur.

Vaux sat down on the floor, back against the green tiled wall, legs stretched out. He had been stupidly naïf to put his trust in a stranger in a small café in a rundown district, frequented by a cosmopolitan group of idlers and misfits. But he had taken the chance when Mustafa had mentioned Dawson's memorable Outback code name. Who else would know it other than an ally on his side? *Time will tell*, he told himself as he felt for the burner phone. It wasn't in his jacket pocket. He searched in the pockets of his tan chinos but only found a few euro coins. There was nothing to do but wait.

He felt a hand grip his shoulder to shake him. He had nodded off.

'Okay, my friend, come with me please,' said a genial man who could have been French. He had short, curly black hair and wore rimless eyeglasses. He was dressed in a blue suit with a white open-collared shirt. He was slightly diminutive, about five-six, and wore black sneakers with a white trim.

Vaux entered a small office on the second floor of the villa. Through french windows, he saw the picture-perfect harbour, bordered by strikingly white cliffs over which squawking seagulls swooped and dived. He couldn't place the location but knew it had to be along the coast from Marseille.

'Monsieur, please sit down,' the genial man said. 'We will not keep you long. I apologize for the method of, shall we say, your transportation.'

'More like an abduction or kidnapping, I should say,' Vaux said dryly.

'You must excuse us. But our security people determined the

method by which we could get you here, unobserved for the most part, and certainly not followed. It was for your own safety, of course.'

Vaux felt compelled to agree. 'Yes, of course. I understand.'

'My name is Francois, by the way. And may I ask how you wish to be addressed? As Mr. Vaux, Monsieur Vaux, or will it be Mr. Westropp?'

'We're all on the same side, I gather. So let's just get on with it. Why am I here? I was told I was to meet my old friend Gerald Dawson.'

'Yes, well that was, 'ow you say? A ruse. Same word in French, non?'

Vaux suddenly felt he could use a drink. 'Tell me, Francois, do you have a drink in your house? A whisky perhaps?'

'*Bien sur. Attendez*, please to wait.'

He left the room. Vaux got up to examine the contents on a desk that had been pushed against the wall adjacent to the french windows. Nothing but a blotter, a few ballpoint pens, and paper clips. But he was sure the room was wired; otherwise, what would be the purpose of the interview, even if between friends and allies?

'Voila,' Francois said as he reentered the room and plunked down a tall glass, half-filled with Scotch and ice cubes.

Vaux gulped it down in one shot. Then he noticed another man hovering behind Francois. He was short, looked decidedly Arab, even though he wore a tight-fitting European suit with a white shirt and open collar. His scuffed black shoes were dusty, as if he had come in from a long walk.

'This is Mahmoud. He is the key to what we are doing here. He will tell you the full story and relate to you why he has decided to come forward at this juncture to forestall—yes? To forestall, or prevent at least, this planned massive terrorist act against his people, the Algerian people, and their religious and political leaders.' He nodded to Mahmoud to signal he should commence his dissertation.

Mahmoud, a slightly built man, went over to an upholstered armchair that had been covered with a dust sheet. Vaux remained standing until Francois pointed his finger at an upright chair by the desk. Vaux sat down and set his empty glass on the desk.

He turned to Mahmoud and said, 'I'm here to listen.'

'Very well, sir. Just so you understand: I am a member of a sleeper cell—I think that's what you would call it—here in Marseille, whose primary allegiance is to a newly formed jihadist alliance between the militant groups known as Boko Haram and Al-Shebaab. I can also tell you that negotiations are now in progress to absorb what remains of the defunct Al-Qaeda in the Islamic Maghreb, known as AQIM.'

Mahmoud paused to take out a loose cigarette and a slim gold lighter from his side pocket. He lit up with the fast skill of a habitual smoker and blew out the first intake from the side of his mouth. Francois gave an impatient cough and walked over to the french windows. He pulled hard but without success.

Mahmoud ignored him. 'So this is the group I am in contact with. They have a plan, sir. A diabolical plan, a conspiracy that should outrage all Muslims across the world. This is why I am here. I am not a traitor or, as I think you say in English, a quisling. No. I am a true Muslim. My faith has come to mean more to me than any political movement. Our religion is to perpetuate love, my friend, not the murder of innocent civilians or the destruction of our holy places.'

Vaux remained silent. He was there to listen.

'And so, my friend, I understand that the information I am about to impart to you may help thwart the diabolical plans of these jihadists. Let us get to the point, non?'

Vaux nodded and leaned forward towards his interlocutor, his elbows on his knees, his chin resting on his clenched fists. 'I am all ears, monsieur.'

'These enemies of God are the same people who killed twenty-one non-believers at the Bardo museum in Tunis last March. They belong to the same group—mostly members of an Algerian ISIL cell who, you may remember, shot up the Paris offices of a political magazine and killed seventeen great journalists.

'Now these bad people have drawn up a diabolical plan to destroy the Djamaa el Djazair mosque, still under construction on the Bay of Algiers and scheduled for completion in 2019. Building started there, with the blessing of God, back in 2009.

'Everything is behind schedule but of course it will be completed eventually. It will be the third biggest mosque in the world—after those of Mecca and Medina. It will be one of the wonders of the world, and it will represent gloriously the nearly two billion Muslims who honour their faith.'

Vaux gestured to Francois, who stood patiently at the door, for another drink. Francois nodded, turned around, and left the room quietly.

'You must understand, monsieur. I put my faith above everything. Without my faith in Mohammed and his teachings, I am nothing. I was brought up to believe, to have faith, and I will die as a believer. I cannot put loyalty to my political allies over the devotion and commitment to my religion, the very core of my existence.

'So that is why, if you forgive this lengthy speech, I am willing to divulge this evil plan to destroy this great and holy project. I am willing to betray my former allies, but mark you, not my faith and not my radicalism to fight for the eventual victory of the Arab peoples in their struggle for respect and justice.'

Vaux fiddled with his empty glass. 'I understand your position. And their motivation is what?'

'To render a heavy blow against Bouteflika and his cronies; they are viewed as a corrupt gang who raped the people of the riches from God's munificent gifts of oil and natural gas. They could have built a paradise after the war of independence from the French colonialists, but instead, they grabbed the people's resources and the country's wealth. The clique that runs the country are all as rich as Croesus.

'Not only that, the building will cost some $1.2 billion by the time it is finished. This money, these AQIM followers argue, could have been better spent on building schools, hospitals, and clinics, the need for which in Algeria is urgent.'

'So your friends—'

'Not my friends, sir. Not my friends.'

'Sorry, these people, this terrorist cell, they are bent on mayhem and destruction, not positive dialogue.'

'Too late for dialogue.'

'But may I ask where we go from here? Are you willing to reveal the names and locations of the members of what you call this sleeper cell? And will you be able to inform us about probable timelines? Do these people have a schedule? And are we talking weeks, months—or next year, for example?'

Mahmoud took a sheet of paper from the inside pocket of his jacket. He got up and gave it to Vaux, who quickly scanned the contents.

'I see. Well, of course, you may rest assured that my people will take immediate action to stop this outrage. I commend you for coming forward. It's a brave act, and apart from salvaging this great project to honour your religion, you've probably saved many lives.'

'*Alhamdulillah*, thanks be to God,' Mahmoud said, sighing.

One floor beneath the room where Vaux had received the briefing, Mishka removed his headset and punched the audio equipment's off button.

'That was quite a speech for a Catholic. Have you managed to convert him?'

'In his spare time, he is a professional actor, sir. But he read a lot,' Mustafa said quietly, happy that he was able to produce the false prophet.

'How long did you say you have known him?'

'Many years, sir. Many years.'

'Well, he did an excellent job. Now organise our guest's departure. And ask our fake Muslim to stay on for dinner.'

Part 2

Chapter 14

In the early part of the twenty-first century, the Middle East, a persistently stagnant and backward region of the modern world, became embroiled in one of the longest and most brutal civil wars in history.

The focus of the conflict was Syria, headed by a ruthless young leader by the name of Bashar al-Assad, who had succeeded his father Hafez al-Assad. Bashar was in his mid-twenties and had been studying in London to become a dentist.

His father, who had showed considerable skill in keeping the various religious and political factions that plagued Syria's fractious politics under control, had died suddenly in June 2010, at the age of sixty-one.

But the tight lid on the pressure cooker of Syrian society had finally blown. The young Bashar promised a new society, social reforms, more trickle-down wealth for the masses, peace among the religious factions.

Not one of those promises was kept. The kleptocratic Assad

regime, together with its sycophantic hangers-on, proved reluctant to share the nation's wealth; an all-out battle was launched against the reformers.

The brutal and bloody conflagration started in 2011 with street protests, a general civil uprising. Armaments trickled in from many quarters, mostly small arms, explosives, and IEDs. The fanatic Islamic State of Iraq and the Levant [ISIL] group seized the opportunity, joined the rebels, and turned the mass uprising into a holy and bloody civil war.

While Syria's young leader sought refuge with his family in the vast marble Presidential Palace and its labyrinthine underground bunkers, the loyal Syrian Air Force bombed many of the country's towns and villages to rubble and choked fleeing refugees with Sarin nerve gas.

By 2015, full-scale civil war had devastated most of the country. Damascus, the capital, had been hit hard, but its administrative core had been left unscathed. The civil and military government continued to operate. Syria, on the point of collapse as the war dragged on, kept up a semblance of normality. The Russians, a traditional ally, stayed firmly loyal to Bashar al-Assad, while the United States hammered both the regime and its ISIL enemies with its vast arsenal of B-52 bombers, AC-130 gunships, F-18 fighter planes, and predator drones.

But Syria's government structures remained intact. With Russia's military support, the regime of Bashar Al-Assad held firm, even though the war's death toll approached three hundred thousand men, women, and children.

Along with the Syrian armed services—mostly recruited from the loyalist Alawite sect—the nation's diplomatic service kept the faith. Assad's ambassadors, consuls general, and myriad diplomatic apparatchiks, including associated spy/intelligence networks, went about their duties on foreign soil as if catastrophe—the total collapse of the regime—was not within the realm of possibility.

Which was why, at this particular time in history, Bruno

Valayer, Syria's long-time honorary consul in Marseille, sat at the bar of his favourite watering hole on the Corniche President Kennedy. From his own reserved pew, marked by a small brass plate screwed to the highly polished mahogany bar, all thoughts, all regrets of that country's current agonies, dissipated into a benign cloud of well-being and, yes, optimism, as he gazed through the large picture windows at the indigo blue of the becalmed Mediterranean.

His fingers stroked the cool, tall stem of the martini glass as he waited patiently for the contact he had so carefully cultivated since learning of his cosmopolitan background, his dubious circle of *mecs*, and his constant need for cash infusions to keep his beloved bar afloat.

Gerald Dawson, wearing his habitual bush hat, a khaki safari jacket, and grubby blue jeans, walked through the gilt-framed glass doors. A few couples sat on overstuffed leather sofas, sipping from champagne glasses, but the man he had come to meet was moored at his usual place at the end of the bar.

He had known Bruno Valayer for some years, and he always reminded Dawson of the French version of some Hollywood idol of the 1940s—with sleeked black hair, a Clark Gable moustache, and the habitual dark blue Savile Row suit that emphasized his slim build.

'How ya going, mate? Forgive my casual attire; just come from a barbie up in the hills.'

'What are you drinking?' Valayer replied. 'You usually like Joe's martinis.'

'Nah, not after that meal. I'll have a Scotch.'

'They only have the malts. Glenfiddich, perhaps?'

Dawson nodded to Joe, the diminutive Italian barman, who had sidled up to the two men to take the order.

'So what's on your very fertile and imaginative mind, mate? *You* called *me*, remember?'

Valayer waited for the barman to pour a double shot of the

tawny malt whisky into a heavy-bottomed old-fashioned glass. Ice cubes came piled in a similar glass.

'The official Syrian consul general here asked me to make a few inquiries, Gerry. His questions led me to the conclusion that the one man in Marseille who could help me is my old and trusted friend, Gerald Dawson.'

'Go on.'

'Well, here's the thing. Naguib, a very conscientious diplomat, is anxious to please his boss, or some higher-up in Damascus.'

'Blimey, are they still functioning?'

'Of course. Even in war, life goes on. Damascus is relatively unscathed. As our Arab friends would say, "Thanks be to Allah."'

'Don't think Allah's got much to do with it. Anyway, go on.'

'At any rate, my superior is anxious to confirm the accuracy of some reports by our various assets in Marseille whether one Michael Vaux, aka Derek Westropp, is alive and well in this great, historic city, and if so, can I shed any light on the rumours swirling around the purpose of his current gig, as they say.'

Dawson took another sip of the malt. He stroked his chin as if trying to recall the name, or even the *nom de guerre.* 'Well, well, now. And what makes you think I even know this individual in the first place? In the second instance, if I did know him, why would I know what the bugger's up to?'

Valayer gave out a theatrical scoff. 'Come on, Gerry, you know everything that's going on in this great city of conspiracies, treachery, and espionage.'

'You must know more than I do, mate. I don't know what you're talking about—'

'That bar of yours is an international exchange of gossip, intelligence, and intrigue, for God's sake. You must have heard something.'

Dawson reflected on the man whose path he crossed perhaps once or twice a year. A strange hybrid type: a UK-educated Frenchman, lucky in love [he had married a wealthy Parisian heiress] and lucky professionally, thanks to an old college friend who had climbed the ranks of Syria's diplomatic service to a point where he could offer him a virtual sinecure—the well-funded but largely inactive posting as Syria's honorary consul in France's second-largest city.

'What's this all about, anyway? You want some gossip about old Vaux, or what?'

'It's nothing too serious. That's why I thought you could help. One of our informants reported seeing you two together at the Bar du Port, that's all. He recognised the man from pictures Syria's GSD had circulated at one time as Enemy Number One. Back in the late '90s, I think.'

'And is he still Enemy Number One?' Dawson asked cautiously.

'I'll tell you the whole story if you can help me track this character down.'

'What, then find him floating in the docks, throat slashed, dead as a dodo?'

'Nothing like that, I assure you. If I understand the story fully, they want to warn him about a plot to expose him for past misdeeds. Something like that. We think it's some weird strategy designed by MI6 high-ups to set a clever trap for him to fall into so they can charge him with betraying the cause. In other words, it looks like he's being set up so they can nab him for past indiscretions and suspected betrayals.'

'A frame-up, in other words. So what do you want from me? I'm not going to intervene in matters of no concern to me. I could end up bloody dead too.' Dawson had lowered his voice as he checked the bar for possible eavesdroppers.

'We know you two go back a few decades—the newspaper business and all that. And besides, the Syrians know perfectly well what your game is—'

'My game's self-survival.'

'Exactly, Gerry. You'll be well compensated, as usual.'

Chapter 15

A bored Patrick Thursfield sat in front of the flickering bluish computer screen in the room above Vaux's flat on the first floor of the tall, shabby safe house on the Rue de Refuge. To relieve his boredom, he had decided to call Olive, the girl who lived in the big Tudor house in Chalk Farm in the northern suburbs of London. They were both occupants, among several other young men and women, of the house that in the sixties had been divided up into several bed-sits. She lived on the ground floor and had promised to keep an eye on Thursfield's studio apartment while he was away, as he had put it, on a top secret assignment.

Suddenly, the monitor came to life. Vaux was entering the apartment. Olive would have to wait. He watched the monitor as Vaux threw off his light linen jacket and went through to the kitchen. Thursfield switched up the volume of the audio system and could hear the steady gurgle of beer being poured into a glass. He saw and heard the door of the mini-fridge slam shut and then observed Vaux go back to the living room. To his astonishment,

Vaux then picked up the rarely used, specially assigned, and monitored BlackBerry on his bedside table and punched in Craw's secret code.

Craw had told Vaux that as soon as he made contact with MI6's Algerian asset, he should inform him so Operation Mascara could be put into full play. Vaux had assumed that once he obtained the identity of the terrorist cell that planned to blow up the mosque, the whole operation would be handled by some UK-French anti-terrorist team, and that would be the end of the evil conspiracy.

Thursfield now adjusted his headset to listen to their conversation.

'Craw.'

'Glad I got hold of you. By my reckoning, it's 5 p.m., your time. Thought you might have left the office by now.'

'Your observation is spot-on, dear boy. What's up?'

'I finally made contact. Our whistle-blower has given me the goods, including the location of the plotters, the cell, if you like.'

'Fantastic. Well done, Vaux. This will be a major coup for B3, what?'

'I feel like a schoolboy asking the headmaster if he can go home now.'

'Stay in place. Await further instructions. Don't want you wandering around Europe where we can't find you. I'll call you early tomorrow.'

Then the line went dead.

Thursfield took the earphones off and watched Vaux stretch out on the narrow bed and fall asleep. Earlier, he had adjusted a tiny spy camera to a crumbling wall frieze opposite the bed. He now had a full view of a splayed-out Vaux; with an erotic twinge, he wondered whether the suspected double agent would soon be joined by the exotic female he had failed to catch on camera on her first visit.

* * *

Vaux slept deeply for about an hour. When he woke up, he felt hungry and in need of a shower. He was moving carefully towards the narrow stand-up shower in the small bathroom when he heard his burner phone give off its familiar ringtone. Naked, he went back to the bed and picked up the smartphone that rested on the small bedside table beside the official and suspect BlackBerry.

'Monsieur Vaux?'

The gruff, Australian-accented French indicated a friendly call from Gerry Dawson. He couldn't remember giving Dawson the phone number and pressed the talk button.

'Yes, mate. What can I do for you?'

'Come on over. I've got someone I want you to meet,' Dawson said, rather abruptly.

Vaux hesitated. He didn't feel inclined to have another assignation with lovely Dominique, as appealing and as friendly as she was. 'Look, Gerry, I'm hungry and a little weary. That's all. I've had a long day and don't feel like partying. Sorry.'

'I've just what the doctor bloody ordered, mate. Come on over and be surprised.'

'Give me fifteen minutes,' Vaux said, surrendering.

Thursfield, screen-struck at the sight of a naked Vaux moving from the shower stall back to the bed, shook his head in frustration as he observed Vaux pick up the uncompromised Apple 6s to talk to the unknown caller. It was all the more exasperating in the wake of the recent call to Craw; he had heard the two men's conversation as clearly and distinctly as if they were both sitting in his own operations room.

* * *

The Bar du Port was unusually quiet for midday. Dawson sat on a tall stool at the zinc bar as if he were a customer; behind the bar, Dominique, in her usual blue jeans and matelot t-shirt, was quietly drying and polishing wine glasses. A man Dawson had never seen before sat at a small table by the side of the staircase that led up to the quiet and unoccupied second-floor guestrooms.

Dawson gazed down at that morning's *Nice Matin* but wasn't reading. Surreptitiously, he looked over at the stranger who was now engrossed in rolling his own cigarette. Like most small bars in Marseille, the no-smoking bylaws were ignored. He was about thirty, Dawson reckoned, dressed in jeans and a leather bomber jacket, and seemed determined not to be sociable, even though he had briefly chatted up Dominique while she served him.

Dawson was now struggling to translate the newspaper's elegant editorial when he heard the rattling of beads as the curtain that covered the entrance was pulled aside by a new customer. It was Vaux.

'How you doing, sport?' Dawson asked as he stood up for a mutual bear hug.

Vaux grabbed a bar stool, but before he could sit down, Dawson gripped his arm and nodded to the narrow staircase that climbed to the upper floors. Dawson held his arm in a friendly, guiding way to the stairs. They passed the stranger, who looked up at them with some curiosity.

Dawson opened the door to the small room Vaux had occupied the night Mishka Arenson had guided him there. Dawson sat down on the only upright chair in the room. It was rickety and had a narrow straw seat too small for Dawson's ample backside.

Vaux had no choice but to sit uncomfortably on the side of the sagging bed. 'What's up?' he asked.

'Keep your voice down, mate. I don't trust that party downstairs,' said Dawson.

'Who?'

'You're a real wanker at times, aren't you, Vaux? The bloody stranger downstairs.'

'Oh. Sorry, I thought he was a customer.'

'Well, he was, wasn't he? Oh, never mind. Listen, mate, I think you're in some sort of trouble, and as an old friend, I just want to warn you of certain happenings around here that may, shall we say, affect you—and not in a good way, either.'

His warning attracted Vaux's interest. 'Go on,' he said.

'Number one: you do know, don't you, that this bloody city is as corrupt as they come? You remember that book by Graham Greene? It was called *J'Accuse*, and it blew the bloody lid off all the corruption and graft going on in Nice at the time. Old Greene, God bless 'im, lived close to Nice on the Cap d' Antibes.

'Well, anyway, never mind about Nice or Cannes; this place takes the biscuit. All sorts of rackets, the mob, the local politicians—they're all here gorging at the trough of corruption and bribery, while the ordinary people are barely living in shoddy townships north of the core, Algerians, Tunisians, Africans, not to mention the poorer French, you name it.'

'What are you leading up to?' Vaux asked, surprised at this sudden concern about civic and social affairs on the part of an old friend, who for as long as he could remember had very little interest in politics or social questions.

'Just so you know, I have many irons in the fire hereabouts, and I'm pretty well tuned in. I think you're being set up, mate. I've heard on the grapevine, for instance, that there could be a plot afoot to ensnare you in some scandal or other. Don't ask me what it's all about. We've never talked about what you've been doing since you were let go by the *Times,* but whatever it is, mate, I think you should keep your bright blue eyes skinned so you can take evasive action before all hell lets loose.'

Vaux was shocked by the intensity of Dawson's conviction. He thought about how to respond without giving his friend any inkling of his mission in Marseille. 'Thanks, Gerry. I really appreciate this concern for me. But I think I know what I'm doing. Yes, it's connected to the government, but nothing that borders on anything that could blow up in my face. It's just a freelance assignment I agreed to take on.'

Dawson looked sceptical. 'Whatever you say. But I've warned you, okay? And now I have something quite specific to tell you.'

'Go on.'

'Again, from my multiple contacts, I've learned that the Syrian consulate here would like you to pay a visit to their offices. They are holding an important message from some government department in Damascus which will be in your best interest to receive—'

'Wait a moment,' he interrupted. 'The Syrians want to communicate with *me*?'

'Yeah, mate. You can take that to the bank. Not just my suspicion or hunch. Someone official asked me to relate their request to get in touch. Phone 'em and make an appointment. The man who asked me to pass on the message is none other than the consul himself. He's their honorary consul here, a fastidious Frenchman, who says he's acting on instructions from Damascus.'

'Walk into a hostile consulate,' Vaux stated calmly, 'and you may never come out. I'm persona non grata with the Syrian government—have been for years.'

'Why's that then?' Dawson asked, genuinely puzzled.

'It's a long story. Briefly, I worked for them in a non-official capacity some years ago—not a journalistic job, more diplomatic. It was arranged through an old college friend. He was a Syrian who later became the head of economic research at the central bank in Damascus. To cut a long story short, they accused me of disloyalty, betrayal, by feeding information—they said "classified" information—to the UK authorities. Which was bunk, of course.

'A few years after that sorry episode, I got entangled with a glamorous Palestinian who, just by chance, worked undercover for MI6. At least I thought she did. It turned out she'd been a double agent for the Syrian intelligence service. At that time, I was doing a bit of freelance work for Department B3, a sort of subsidiary operation connected to MI6's Mideast and North Africa desk.

'Complications led to further difficulties and entanglements, and the Syrians suspected I had forged this romantic relationship solely to spy on their intelligence activities. Overnight, I was branded persona non grata by the Syrians, and the romance came to an abrupt end.'

Dawson looked sceptical. 'And all this happened while you were working for the newspapers and weeklies?'

'I had no choice. Queen and country and all that.'

Dawson sighed. 'Truth to tell, I've done a bit of that clandestine work myself. But I stick to an old rule in the Great Game: keep clear of the floozies. They only bring trouble.'

'The Palestinian girl in question was no floozy,' said Vaux.

'I read somewhere that women make the best spies. Anyway, let's go.'

When both men trundled noisily down the uncarpeted staircase, the stranger, a scrawny cigarette dangling from his lips, was quickly gathering his possessions together. Dawson would later swear he saw him squirrel a small metallic object into his jacket pocket. It looked to him like one of those micro-cameras as small as a flash drive he had seen Alan Craw play with when they had met occasionally to liaise, as Craw always put it. But by now, the chain-smoking stranger had left the bar.

* * *

Vaux walked towards the Old Port area and turned right on the Quai de Rive Neuve. He took a deep breath; the harbour air was invigorating—an exotic mix of pure ozone and the odor of the early morning's fish catch from the stalls that lined the harbour's edge. He felt he needed a long walk to digest what Dawson had told him. His first thought was to retrieve his Sig Sauer P226 from the items he had stashed in the locker at the Gare St. Charles.

He crossed the tree-lined, historic Canebiere, a street that had once rivaled the Champs Elysees as France's most elegant boulevard but in recent years had been largely neglected by the city planners. Now its historic grandeur had faded into a traffic-jammed thoroughfare lined by ailing, leafless plane trees and shabby buildings. When he reached the Vieux Port metro station he got into a waiting taxi. He sank into the back seat, and as he pulled the door closed, he saw a man dart into the cab behind his. He was the chain-smoking stranger at the Bar du Port.

So he was being followed. Whoever the pavement artist [Note 7] worked for, he could only guess. But it wouldn't be hard to shake him off in these tortuous madcap streets. Within a few minutes, his confidence was justified.

The cab driver, spurred by Vaux's telling him he was late for his Paris-bound TGV, suddenly swerved right into a narrow one-way side street, ignored a light that had turned red, and sped across the busy Cours Franklin D. Roosevelt, then dove into a maze of narrow, clogged side streets whose general direction headed northeast to the Gare St. Charles.

Within a few minutes, the old, battered Citroen had come to a halt behind a line of waiting taxis. Vaux searched for change but he had none, so the driver smiled at the outsize tip in euro notes. The sight of the imposing Gare St. Charles, with its columned Acropolis-like structure, somehow comforted Vaux. Perhaps it was the first sign of homesickness. From there, after all, he could get on a TGV and within a few hours travel through France and then zoom under the English Channel and on to London.

Vaux shook off his pang of nostalgia, got out of the taxi and rushed up the broad, shallow steps of the Gare St. Charles, remembered the location of the left-luggage lockers and turned in the opposite direction towards a crowded concourse lined with fast-food outlets and boutiques. He bought an *Americana* at the Starbucks outlet and sat on a tall stool at the window that looked on to the crowds rushing to their trains or milling around to kill time. He watched for his tail for about twenty minutes and then left to retrieve the Sig Sauer P226.

Chapter 16

They arranged to meet at a harbour-side restaurant called La Souk. The terrace, sheltered by a white awning with gold stripes, looked out to a bobbing forest of sailboat masts and, across the port to the south bank, the Quai Rive Neuve. Dawson, impatient with Vaux's hesitancy, had acted as middleman in the negotiations, and he now sat far back in the inside of the restaurant chatting to the chef and part-owner, a slim, short Moroccan known among his clientele as Ali Baba.

For mutual recognition, Vaux had said he would be ostentatiously reading the latest edition of *Charlie Hebdo*, in honour of the magazine's journalists killed by terrorists in early 2015. Such was his state of mind at the thought, the very thought, that finally, after all the ill-will and recriminations, Damascus had finally expressed a wish to communicate with him.

Over the top of his steel-rimmed reading glasses, Vaux sensed a shadowy figure approaching. This is it, he thought. He didn't look up from the magazine as he heard a chair scraping the tiled floor and felt the table rock slightly as a slim man nestled into the cane chair opposite.

'Monsieur Westropp, I presume,' said the stranger.

Vaux looked up. For some reason, the use of his nom de guerre took him unawares. But he quickly recovered. 'Oui, monsieur. And you, I presume, are Monsieur Bruno Valayer.'

'*Oui, en effet*—exactly,' said Valayer.

The elegance of the Syrian envoy, his pomaded hair and his thin pencil moustache, reminded Vaux of the movie portrayals of Hercule Poirot, Agatha Christie's indomitable detective. He decided to say very little. After all, the honorary consul had asked for the meeting.

A young waiter emerged from the back of the restaurant to take their orders. Valayer asked to see the wine list. Vaux ordered a Heineken.

'Well, Monsieur Westropp. So nice of you to agree to see me.'

'Yes,' said Vaux.

Valayer smiled, noted Vaux's coldness but ploughed on with the business at hand. 'This won't take long.' He paused while the waiter put down Vaux's beer.

Valayer quickly scanned the wine list. 'Bring me a glass of your Mouton-Cadet, chilled.'

The waiter wrote the order on a pad, turned, and hurried to the bar in the back of the restaurant.

'Well, now Monsieur Westropp. At last we meet. I have, over the years, heard a lot about you.'

'No doubt. I understand you are anxious to give me some information or some message from the Syrian side.' Vaux knew he was sounding unfriendly, even pompous, but he wanted to get the meeting over and done with.

'Oh yes. All in good time. I am French-born, you know, and we like to take the diplomatic path, 'ow you say?—well, rather cautiously. Let's not plunge into the business talk before we 'ave, what I think they say in the best circles, a libation.'

Vaux signaled his agreement by taking a swig from the bottle of Heineken.

It was a sunny morning, but an autumnal chill—a foretaste of the seasonal mistral, perhaps—blew in from north of the harbor, and some of the quayside cafés had put on overhead electric space heaters for the customers who preferred to sit on the outside terraces.

After a respectful silence, Bruno Valayer came to the point. 'I have been instructed, by the Syrian authorities, to request your cooperation in a certain matter they regard as quite urgent.'

Valayer then produced an envelope from the inside of his blue linen jacket. 'You can read it at your leisure. I will tell you the nub of the matter: Alena Hussein, a senior member of our foreign affairs secretariat, wishes urgently to communicate with you on matters of what she calls mutual interest.'

Vaux, who had been sipping from his bottle, put it down with a thud. His eyes fixed on Valayer as if to reassure himself that he had heard right. 'A voice from the dead. I haven't heard from her for over a decade.

'I thought she had been swallowed up in the massive bureaucracy of Syrian's intelligence apparatus—or worse, had met the same fate as my old friend Ahmed Kadri, who died some years ago while under interrogation by your security people.'

Valayer looked shocked, visibly taken aback by Vaux's offensive allegations. He remained silent as he composed his reply. 'Syria is no worse than most countries playing on the Mideast chessboard, Monsieur. But this is not the time for a political discussion. My duty is to relay the official message: Madame Alena Hussein wishes to contact you. I have the means, very secure, that will facilitate the conversation she wishes to have, face to face, if you so desire. A highly secure and encrypted video system has recently been installed by Damascus to communicate with all its outposts. It is totally cyber-safe, as they say these days. I'm not a technical man, but if you want to check, I think the system'—here, Valayer deftly read from a fragile piece of paper he had fished from his top pocket—'is based on what is known as the impenetrable Rijndael principle.' Then he spelled it out: 'R.I.J.N.D.A.E.L.'

Vaux was none the wiser. But his pulse quickened at the thought of possibly seeing Alena once more and perhaps arranging a clandestine meeting and then hugging her with the close affection, even love, he still felt for her. They spent years together in Cairo, when she was acting second secretary at the Syrian embassy and he worked as the bureau chief of a Damascus-based English-language newspaper; the memories of that time together were burned into his soul, his very being. Perhaps they were the happiest years of his life.

Vaux shook himself awake from what he later thought was probably a trance, a reverie brought on by mental shock. 'Yes, Monsieur Valayer. We should arrange a date and time for this to go ahead.'

'The necessary mechanisms are located in the consulate building on Rue Paradis. Do you know the area? It's east of the harbour, close to the Musée Cantini.'

'I can find it,' said Vaux.

'Then may I suggest the day after tomorrow. Say at 9 a.m.?' Valier handed Vaux his embossed business card.

For a moment, Vaux wondered if he was walking into a trap. But then he said, 'Yes, fine. I'll see you then.'

Valayer noisily pushed his chair back, stood up, and threw a twenty-euro bill on the table. Vaux stood, and both men shook hands. Vaux then turned around to see if Dawson was still there. The room was empty. Vaux walked out to the street, turned right and headed west, towards the Musée de Docks Romain. There, in a small café where he sipped an espresso, he thought about the ancient seafaring Romans, their ephemeral love lives, and the generations that followed.

* * *

'It's all here in black and white, thanks to Jimmy Dean,' said an enthusiastic Thursfield.

It was early morning, and he was talking to Alan Craw, who at ten o'clock had just seated himself at his desk at Department B3's offices on Gower Street.

'Who the hell's Jimmy Dean?' asked a bewildered Craw.

'Just to remind you, sir, you did say I have permission to act independently when required, hire my own contacts and cut-outs, etc.'

'Yes, yes, go on.'

'Well, I asked a freelance photographer friend of mine to trail Vaux, and he's come up trumps, sir. I have actual photos of him in full color talking to the Australian caretaker—'

'You mean Outback, don't you?'

'Yes, sir.'

'Well, let's keep to the code names, please.'

'Yes, sir, but this *is* the secure phone.'

'Go on, Thursfield. Get to the point.'

'Well, sir, yesterday, we he hit the jackpot. I have several shots of Vaux talking to a known Syrian operative on the terrace of a restaurant in the Old Port. My hired hand just sat in the back seat of a cab outside the place and kept clicking his miniature spy camera. We have over twenty pictures of Vaux liaising with, as I say, a known Syrian asset.'

Craw did not reply. This was the breakthrough he had been waiting for—proof that Vaux was talking to the Syrians and no doubt warning them that Anglo-French security was on to the plot to blow up the half-finished Algiers mosque. And that the anti-terrorist squad was biding its time before executing the raid and the subsequent destruction of the militant group.

Vaux had taken the bait. The Syrians would now struggle to contact the phony terrorist sleeper cell and caution them to abandon the current plan and wait for another opportunity. This was all he needed to charge Vaux as a co-conspirator, arrest him in France, and bring him back for an espionage trial that would, he hoped, inevitably lead to a lengthy prison term in the Scrubs, the storied jail reserved for traitors and fellow travellers.

Craw felt the gratifying sensation of a battle finally won. And he could not suppress a rather sadistic smile at the thought of Anne, doing service to queen and country all these months as she stoically stayed away from her lover Vaux, finally giving up on him as he languished in jail at Her Majesty's pleasure.

Thursfield waited patiently for his boss to congratulate him for his initiative in hiring his own joe. But there was silence at the other end of the line as Craw mulled over his options.

'I want you to leave things just as they are,' Craw finally said. 'I'll be coming over within a day or so. I want to be in on the kill, you understand. Meanwhile, continue to keep close tabs on our quarry. The more evidence we have of Vaux's collusion with those bastards, the more ammunition we have to lock him away and out of harm's way for a long time to come. Understand, my boy?'

'Yes, sir,' Thursfield said dutifully.

Chapter 17

Craw couldn't contain his excitement at the success of the entrapment plan that would finally seal his rival's fate. He savoured the outcome as if it had been a classical battle won by the side that represented the good versus the evil geniuses who constantly tried to defeat the God-fearing Western world.

Vaux, he had no doubt, was part of the squalid conspiracy that constantly worked against the interests of the UK and its allies in the West. The West had made mistakes, but the post-WWII alliance was on the right side of history. The final apprehension of Michael Vaux, the exposure of a man who, Craw had been convinced for a long time, was an Arab lover whose political sympathies had always been for the revolutionary forces that had brought to power the likes of Syria's ruthless Bashir Assad, Iraq's megalomaniac Sadam Hussein, and Libya's madcap Muammar Gaddafi.

Now Mr. Vaux, the insidious former journalist, was about to meet his ignominious end. Craw had always viewed journalists as meddlesome interlopers. He saw the gentlemen and even the ladies of the press as virtual agents provocateurs, at times virtual saboteurs of the West's honourable efforts for world peace.

Number one on his to-do list was a friendly call to Bill Oxley, Vauxhall's chief spy-catcher.

'Bill,' he began jovially. 'Some good news.'

'That's a welcome change. What is it?'

'Operation Mascara is about to wind up. We have been 100 per cent successful.'

Oxley had been hardened by nearly forty years of over-the-top optimism voiced by a succession of underlings and minor aides-de-camp. 'Please elaborate, old boy.'

Craw replied, 'We have irrefutable evidence that our target has been in recent contact with active agents of the non-friendly country we suspect he's been working for these many years on several of our key operations. Our suspicions, after all, were fully justified. In short, we've got 'im by the short and curlies.'

'If I read your artfully coded words correctly, you're telling me that we have caught a suspected double agent red-handed—in communication with the enemy?'

'Absolutely, sir. I trust I have your approval for winding this whole deal up within a day or so. I plan to supervise his arrest on French soil and bring him back as soon as possible to face the music.'

'Yes, of course. I think you'd better clear it with Sir Nigel—after all, he's your immediate chief.'

'Of course. No question. He'll be happy to see the final resolution of the whole matter. For some reason, he has always been reluctant to share my suspicions about one of our own team. But now, of course, it's irrefutable.'

'Well done, Craw. Go to it. Of course, this means a long investigative process to assess the damage this man Vaux has done over the years. Good God. It boggles the mind.'

* * *

Having got the unenthusiastic go-ahead from a preoccupied Sir Nigel, Craw put his long-planned expulsion plan into effect. He would summon the help of the Royal Air Force and request the aid of the Royal Military Police in the actual mechanics of the traitor's arrest. He asked for at least three sturdy members of the RMP's Close Protection Unit [CPU] who would make the arrest and then escort the prisoner back to the UK to face justice. The appropriate French authorities, of course, would be notified of the British exfiltration operation, according to current diplomatic protocol.

* * *

The team flew on an RAF Boeing C-17 short-range transport aircraft from London to the military base at Istres-Le Tube in the south of France, about sixty kilometres north-west of Marseille. They then boarded a French military helicopter that touched down on a tight security area within the precincts of Marseille's international airport.

Craw's interest in the logistics of settling his team in appropriate accommodations was limited to a goodbye and thank-you gesture as he piled into a waiting limo that took him swiftly to the hotel of his choice—the five-star Hotel Dieux, whose big, luxurious rooms looked south over the yacht-crammed Old Port.

* * *

Meanwhile, Vaux lost no time in pursuing the woman he had loved back in those halcyon days after he retired from the newspaper rat race, only to be quickly honeytrapped into serving Her Majesty's Secret Service. He told himself his assignment in Marseille was over; after all, he had passed on to Craw and company the vital information of the planned terrorist attack on Algeria's Djamaa el Djazair mosque, and he had nothing more to do.

In his cramped safe flat on the Rue de Refuge, he quickly finished several classic novels that he had been meaning to read all his life. The page-turning sessions filled the gaps between going out to eat at small cafés, visiting Le Bar du Port, and walking around the busy, touristy Old Port area.

Since handing over the easily acquired fact sheet on the sleeper cell's plans to blow up the grand mosque in central Algiers, he had heard nothing from Craw or anyone else connected to MI6's Department B3. His movements around his cramped room and the small kitchen were duly monitored by Thursfield in his audio/video operation room a floor above. Thursfield's overall ennui and boredom, if Vaux could only have known, probably exceeded his own.

Rue Paradis runs in a north-south direction east of the Old Port, a long elegant boulevard whose classic balconied ochre buildings and wide sidewalks were shaded by big plane and sycamore trees. Vaux took an old, rather shaky elevator to the second floor. He sat in an austere anteroom where French newspapers and weekly magazines were scattered on a highly polished, long walnut table. He picked up the latest European edition of *Time* and flipped through the glossy pages.

After ten minutes, he heard steps approach the glass-topped door, saw a man's blurry image through the frosted glass, and then Bruno Valayer, Syria's honorary consul in the port city of Marseille, stood before him. He was elegantly dressed in a grey lightweight suit, a silk white shirt, black tie, with narrow diagonal gold stripes.

'Vaux, mon ami. Please come.' He beckoned Vaux to follow him down a narrow corridor, lined with sepia pictures of nineteenth-century Damascus, to his office. 'I 'ope you 'ave not been waiting long?'

'No. Just arrived, actually.' Vaux felt nervous juices churn in his stomach. He was unsettled by the thought of seeing Alena after all these years of separation. He felt more anxious than he had expected.

'I have, what I think you say in English, bad news and good news,' Valayer said with a reassuring smile. 'The bad news is that our super-secure video set-up is somehow non-functional this morning. The good news is that the audio system *is* working, efficiently and securely. Your conversation with Alena Hussein will be absolutely secure, protected, and safeguarded. So shall I proceed to make contact?'

Vaux was disappointed. He had rather looked forward to seeing Alena, all these years later. Had she changed? Put on weight? Or had she maintained that young figure, the long black hair that fell to her shoulders? But he also felt relieved. Her voice alone would be comforting, and perhaps that was all he could wish for.

He heard himself say, 'It's perfectly all right. I'll be happy just to have a few words with her.'

'Of course. I shall leave you to it.' Valayer pointed to the grey, flat contraption. 'You can turn up the volume if you wish. But you can also use the earphones. It's up to you.'

Vaux chose the two earplugs. Valayer then left the room. The sleek grey phone then gave out a short buzz.

'Hello. Michael?' Vaux felt his heart jump.

'Yes, Alena. I'm here.'

'Darling. How are you?'

Vaux steeled himself to adopt a businesslike tone, an attempt to steer away from what could easily become a maudlin, nostalgic trip down memory lane. 'I understand you have some message to convey.'

He knew he sounded officious and cold. But it was the only approach he thought appropriate.

Alena chuckled. 'Who told you that? There is no message, darling. I just knew you were in Marseille on one of your clandestine jobs, and since I am now in France, I thought you might want to get in touch.'

'Well, yes, of course. It's nice of you to still think of me—'

'Every day, every night,' she said in a lowered voice tinged with regret.

There was a pause. Vaux felt embarrassed, awkward. Where could this lead? It was foolish for him to agree to talk to one of Syria's emissaries. Syria was not deemed a friendly country by the UK or its allies. The country's leaders were hand in glove with the Putin regime, and although they claimed to be fighting the same Middle East terrorists as the West, for the Syrian regime, it was more a struggle to maintain its ruthless grip on power.

Finally, he said, 'Where are you?'

'I'm in Paris, darling. We could meet—secretly, of course. I am staying at the Westin, the old Intercontinental, on the Rue Castiglione, opposite the Meurice. You could put up at the Grand on Place Opera. I'll deal with the bookings. Noms de guerre, of course.'

'I'm not sure that's such a good idea, Alena. Not at this moment, anyway.'

'Then I shall get straight to the point. You're being set up, Michael. We have it from very reliable sources within your own government that your current project is a façade—if that's the right word—a ruse to incriminate you. There's a cabal at Vauxhall Cross that is convinced you've been a double agent all these years. They've researched your assignments from the days we were involved together in Geneva—remember?—and someone, somewhere has built up a dossier of evidence against you. Our Cairo affair confirmed their suspicions, and they have worked on their project diligently ever since.'

'Cairo affair?' Vaux tried to grasp the meaning of what she was saying.

'Oh, Michael, have you forgotten already?'

'No, no. I never looked upon it as an affair. We saw each other a lot. We didn't live together. We had to maintain a certain separation just because you had a top job with the GSD. I was a humble journalist.'

'Yes, but for an influential Damascus daily. You were being groomed, but you didn't know it.'

'Groomed? Is that why they wanted me back in Damascus so suddenly? Is that why they arrested Ahmed Kadri, my old friend from university days, a former respected official of Assad's regime whom they later hanged for treason?

'I suppose I should be grateful that it was you who warned me I could face the same fate as Ahmed if I returned to Damascus. It was you, remember, who warned me *not* to return to Damascus, to get out of Cairo as quickly as possible.'

'Don't let's argue,' said Alena. 'It's water under the bridge. I want you to see the evidence I have in black and white, Michael. You are in extreme danger. A cabal—shall I call it that?—within your own service has hatched a diabolical plot to ensnare you, blame you for traitorous activities throughout your career as an MI6 operative.

'You've been chasing phantoms down there, darling. We keep tabs on all these terrorist cells and the plots they may be hatching. And nothing, *nothing* bad is by any means imminent. It's a cooked-up conspiracy to see if you get in touch with any agency or government who could be in the know and then warn the terrorist cell that the Brits, aided by the Israelis, are on to it.

'And since you seem to be free to walk around and do whatever pleases you, why can't you just jump on a TGV and have a weekend in glorious Paris? No one need see us together. I could come to your hotel or vice versa. Darling, it could be a matter of life and death. Or perhaps I exaggerate. It's a matter of your future, *n'est-ce pas*? An unjust frame-up could send you away for years.'

*

Alena Hussein, aka Veronica Belmont, aka Barbara Boyd, had walked into the offices of MI6 some fifteen years earlier and had presented herself as a Palestinian refugee who wanted to work for Britain in its fraught dealings with the Middle East. She was in fact the Syrian-born daughter of an émigré student who had studied medicine at London's Charing Cross Hospital. Syria's intelligence service had kept tabs on the family, and finally the GSD [Note 8] had directed her to work as an undercover agent within Britain's Secret Intelligence Service.

Impressed with her fluency in Arabic, French, and English and her economics degree from London's King's College, the mandarins at the rundown Century House headquarters of MI6 had passed her on to the Mideast and North Africa desk, where she was promptly transferred to Department B3, the specialist group of field agents whose vague mandate was to act independently and heroically in areas where veteran MI6 staff feared to tread.

Her subsequent career of betrayal and treachery against those British agent runners who gave her space, security, and liberty became apocryphal. But before the unforeseen debacle, she had been ordered to persuade Vaux, then an ex-journalist contemplating a long retirement and only nebulously patriotic, to come to the aid of the country. Some of B3's detractors called it a 'honeytrap' operation. But as Vaux always told his supporters, he genuinely did fall in love with this beautiful, exotic, and talented olive-skinned Arab.

* * *

Now here he was: nearly fifteen years later, still at the receiving end of her seductive voice, her feminine powers of persuasion, her tenebrous allure. His mind raced as he tried to sort out the repercussions of a sudden trip to Paris. He had completed his assignment. Craw had told him to wait on further instructions but was vague about when he could leave the theatre of operations. What would two or three days matter? It was human to want a break. And the relative proximity of vibrant Paris would surely be seen as an understandable desire to get away from the war zone for a few days.

After a long pause, during which Vaux swore he heard a few telling clicks, he said, 'You haven't lost your powers of persuasion.'

'It's a deal, then?'

'I'll get the early morning train on Saturday.'

Chapter 18

Craw found that he enjoyed the duty, or the burden, of holding a fellow man's fate in his hands. And perhaps breaking that fragile thread that guaranteed a man's mental freedom and physical liberty. It wasn't so much the power that he now wielded over Michael Vaux that filled him with a glowing satisfaction; it was the *poetic* justice of it all—the final comeuppance of a long-time rival, a languid, nonchalant competitor who not only outshone his own professional career but outwitted him in the pursuit of beautiful, sexy Anne.

Vaux had outmanoeuvred or outcharmed him at every turn. But for Vaux, he knew it would have been easy to snap up this glittering trophy wife and spend the rest of his career with her at his side, mingling amid the upper echelons of Kensington's elite mandarin classes.

He was sipping a martini in his big room overlooking the Old Harbour. It was a calm, warm evening, and the lights of the Notre Dame basilica across the harbour to the south flickered like glittering diamonds. He heard a buzz and knew his expected visitor had arrived—as usual, promptly at the appointed time.

He got up and opened the mahogany double doors. Before him stood Mishka Arenson. He was wearing his usual leather bomber jacket with a white turtleneck sweater and baggy blue jeans. His sneakers were scuffed and dusty.

Craw clasped his hands, ushered him in, and asked him what his poison was.

'I'll have a very small whisky. Malt, if you have it.'

'Oh, yes. This bar has everything, old boy. A Glenlivet?'

'Excellent. No ice.'

Craw poured a generous shot of the malt into a cut glass tumbler.

'Mazel tov,' Mishka said, raising his glass to Craw.

'Yes, cheers, old boy,' returned Craw.

Mishka thought he looked impatient to get on with the business at hand.

'Well, Mish, I'm sure you've heard the news.'

'I heard just yesterday that our quarry has been seen talking to the Syrian side. To whom exactly, I don't know. But it seems now you have good reason to go ahead and detain him and finally lay charges. My job's done, I'm happy to say. I'm going back to Paris to collect my wife and then home to Tel Aviv.'

Mishka had sat down heavily in an overstuffed white leather armchair, an incongruous replica of Hollywood circa 1935.

'Good, good. You deserve it.'

'I didn't do too much for Operation Mascara. You were the key man, as it should be.'

'Nonsense; you laid the vital framework. Your Mossad team gave out the first alarm about Vaux's true loyalties. And your work here convinced Vaux he was on to something big, that there really was a plot to blow up the mosque. It's probably the only way we could have finally nailed him.'

They both sipped their drinks, savouring the ultimate success of Operation Mascara.

Then Craw got up and looked through the open french windows. 'That neo-Byzantine basilica, perched on the hill over there, is stunningly beautiful on a dark night like this. You don't light up your synagogues, do you?'

'Sometimes,' said Mishka.

An awkward silence ensued. Finally, Mishka stood up and shook his head at Craw's silent invitation for a refill.

'I must be getting back to Cassis.'

'Shall I ask the concierge to call a taxi?'

'No, no. Mustafa is waiting for me outside.'

At the open double doors, he gave Craw a warm hug. '*L'chaim*,' Mishka said, almost inaudibly. Then with a slight limp, he marched down the wide carpeted corridor towards the bank of elevators.

* * *

In a single window seat on the 6 a.m. TGV from Marseille to Paris, Vaux whipped through the cumbersome Saturday edition of the *New York Times International*. The headlines were as depressing as the early-morning fog that blanketed the late-September landscape flying past his misted window. The newspaper reported that in a raid against Taliban guerillas in Afghanistan, US airplanes had accidentally bombed and killed one hundred patients at a hospital run by Doctors Without Borders in Kabul, Afghanistan; in Ankara, one hundred civilians had been killed by two bomb explosions during civil demonstrations. The Turkish government blamed Kurdish rebels. And in Israel, thirty-two Palestinians and seven Israelis were shot during demonstrations at the Al-Aqsa mosque on the Temple Mount in Jerusalem.

But Vaux did not need the grey weather or the gloomy headlines to depress him. After the first elation at getting out of Marseille and heading for Paris—always a romantic city in his personal history—the excitement waned as he remembered what had triggered the sudden trip.

Alena had warned him he was in dire trouble and that sinister forces were conspiring against him; his own safety was at risk from some obscure plot to expose his loyalties to the enemies of Britain and its Western allies. How in hell does it all make sense?

He decided to look for an old, shabby hotel close to the Gare de Lyon, where he and Ahmed Kadri had stayed as students on the first night of their long-ago post-graduation trip to France. It was nostalgia, all over again. But so what? Paris was essentially a city of reminiscence and longing.

More by instinct than memory, he walked north out of the hectic railway terminus, turned left on the Rue de Lyon, and saw the faded, shabby edifice of the Hotel du Sud.

Later, when he was trying to sort out the sequence of macabre events that day, it became obvious that he had ignored the first basic tenet of the tradecraft they had drummed into him during that brief, perfunctory training course at Portsmouth: to constantly surveil the people around you and if they seem suspicious take evasive action—like quickly disappearing in a nearby loo, or a taxi with a fast-thinking, cooperative driver.

He stood in the small lobby and paid for two nights in cash. He used the Derek Westropp passport, although it probably didn't give him much security. A pimply-faced youth grabbed his leather holdall and took him up to the third floor, where he opened the narrow door and waved his arm in a grand gesture that invited Vaux to survey the small, cramped room. Vaux gave the boy a two-euro coin and plunked his bag in front of the dusty chintz-draped french windows that looked over the narrow street. His thoughts dwelt on all his past visits to the City of Light, sweeping memories triggered by the familiar cries, shouts, and whistles from the street, the muffled car horns, the harsh pop-pop of motor scooters.

The clanging ringtone of his official BlackBerry brought him back to the present. Craw, or whoever it was, would have to wait.

He filched a new burner out of his holdall and dialed the number for the Westin. He wondered what name she had registered under. If she was a legitimate diplomat, a plenipotentiary, as she had described herself, she could be using her real name. So he asked for Ms. Alena Hussein. He got straight through.

''Ello?'

'Mademoiselle Hussein?'

'Michael! So you made it.'

'Yes. But I have a few errands to make. Could we meet at around 7 p.m.? And if so where do you suggest?'

'Why not your place, at the Grand?'

Vaux hesitated. 'Can I suggest an alternative to our respective hotels?'

'You mean where you could plant a few listeners or, God forbid, bodyguards?' She laughed to confirm she was joking.

'Perhaps the Tour d'Argent?' Vaux suggested, skirting her question.

'Enormously expensive—and besides, you have to book weeks in advance.'

'I'm sure there are ways of getting around that,' said Vaux.

'Not on our salaries, darling. Or is your swindle sheet unlimited?'

They discussed the wisdom of being seen together in public. But perhaps the very thought of their reunion, the surprise confirmation of their old relationship, had an opiate effect on their habitual professional caution. They chose not to discuss such mundane questions of security. They were in Paris, after all, and true to form, the city of love and romance offered a tentative rebirth of their shared obsessions.

So they quickly settled on a small bistro Vaux remembered on the Rue Capucine, a narrow cobbled street dominated by a bronze statue of Edward VII, the roué, Paris-loving English king, proudly mounted on a large steed. It was only five minutes' walk from the Grand Hotel, so the venue gave some credence to his having registered there.

He arrived first and waited outside the bistro for a likely taxi. But she came on foot, her arms open wide in surprise and welcome. She really hadn't changed: slim, shoulder-length black hair, tight jeans, white silk shirt, and black pumps with high heels that clicked on the cobblestones. They air-kissed and then hugged each other like old friends.

Large gilt-framed mirrors covered one wall of the bistro. Alena chose to sit on the leather banquette with her back to the mirror so that she could face him while surveilling the busy and noisy restaurant at her leisure. Vaux occasionally glanced up at the mirror behind her. He noticed two men sitting directly opposite. Both had the short-cropped hair of law officers and hoods, and both wore tight-fitting blue suits with white shirts open at the neck. Between lulls in his conversation with Alena, Vaux strained to detect their chosen language. They were talking Arabic with the same guttural Levantine accent he recognised from his days in Damascus.

Suddenly, he realised she was asking what he had chosen to eat. A short, dark waiter in a long white apron hovered at the table, pen and notepad in hand.

It was *gigot d'agneau* for Vaux. Claiming little appetite, Alena opted for the *saumon fumé* starter only. At Vaux's insistence, they ordered a bottle of Beauget-Jouette, an obscure champagne from a small vineyard near Epernay, whose owner befriended Vaux on one of his visits to France in his penniless student days.

The conversation between the two former lovers was polite and halting. Physically, he thought, she hadn't changed that much. Perhaps a little heavier in the face, deeper lines around the glistening hazel eyes. He had wanted to ask her how on earth she could work for an international pariah like Bashar Assad, but they came to a tacit agreement not to talk of politics and destiny until later, when both knew they would retreat to somewhere more discreet and intimate.

Vaux paid cash, and they rose to leave. The two Arabs averted their eyes as they walked past them. Outside on the narrow pavement, Vaux looked for a taxi.

'Your place or mine?' she asked, laughing.

Vaux had rehearsed his answer. 'It's a long time since I saw the old Intercontinental, so let's go to your place.'

'Yes, that's the old name for the Westin. Opposite the Meurice, *n'est-ce pas?*'

'Yes, the former Nazi headquarters where General Choltitz, the military governor of Paris, stayed during the occupation.'

They rode the gilded, mirrored elevator to the sixth floor. She touched her electronic key on the door's sensor, and they entered a large suite whose tall windows overlooked the busy Rue de Rivoli and the manicured *Tuileries* gardens.

'Get yourself a drink, darling. I'm getting into something more comfortable.' Alena disappeared into her bedroom. Vaux moved over to the small bar and found a bottle of Cutty Sark. He poured a generous measure into a tall glass and moved to the windows. Paris glittered in the moonless night, the traffic frenetic but muted within the thick walls and plush carpeted floors of the old hotel.

Alena came out of her room, wrapped in a silk polka-dot dressing gown and nothing else. She wore nothing on her feet except red nail polish. She sat on her curled legs on an overstuffed sofa.

'So what shall we talk about?' she asked.

'You got into contact with me, darling. You said we had to talk because you had discovered I was in danger of falling into some trap, a conspiracy against me—a frame-up, perhaps orchestrated by my own side. Is that right?'

'Yes, of course. Our people have learned that the Brits have invented some cock-and-bull story about a terrorist plot to blow up the big mosque that's now under construction in Algiers. So far, they have failed to identify the sleeper cell, as they call it, or the affiliation the terrorists may have with any other group operating in the region—North Africa and, of course, the French Riviera.'

Alena now looked to see what effect her words had on her former lover. But he continued to sip his drink and look into the middle distance, legs stretched out before him.

'As I'm sure you know, we are in contact with all the relevant militant groups around the Mediterranean basin and points south and east. Assad is fighting hard against the likes of ISIS, AQIM, and al-Shabaab. We are as much against their nefarious activities and atrocities as the West—as your people or the French and Washington—'

Vaux had heard enough. 'Really, Alena, you're beginning to sound like an Assad flack. Let's just agree that we work for opposing sides and drop the bullshit about common enemies. I thought tonight was a private reunion, not a political seminar.'

'I apologize for perhaps a long-winded preamble, darling. To get to the point: I think your side is engaged in an elaborate hoax. They—Craw and his friends—want to see who you share the results of your investigations with, your diligence in tracking down who's responsible for this so-called plot against the Algerian regime. Or even perhaps if you attempt to warn the terrorists that British intelligence is right on their tail.'

'And why would you be interested in telling me all this? It's years since we were together. Those Cairo days were the happiest of my life. In love with you, in love with that ancient city, even in love with my job.'

'Just be careful, Michael—'

Then it happened.

The double doors to the suite crashed open. The two men Vaux had observed in the restaurant on the Rue Capucine rushed towards him, handguns pointing to his chest. Vaux put up his hands in surrender. He saw Alena rush to the double doors to close them. Then she walked quickly to her en suite bedroom and slammed the door closed.

One of the attackers stood behind Vaux, tied a gag around his mouth, noisily stripped duct tape off its spool and bound his arms straight to his body. The other assailant quickly pulled a hood over his head. Vaux then heard the unzipping of a bag and the clink and clank of various heavy tools being laid out on the marble-topped mini-bar.

But then the double doors smashed open again, with a resounding thud. Vaux heard four muffled shots, followed by gasps and heavy thumps as his two assailants fell to the floor. Almost instantaneously, he felt the hood being pulled off his head. Then he saw the two intruders sprawled on the thick-piled blue Aubusson carpet, blood pumping out of their chests and head wounds.

But the shock of seeing the two thugs gunned down in cold blood was nothing compared to the exhilaration he felt when he recognised his unexpected saviour.

Gerald Dawson stood before the grizzly scene, slightly out of breath, his Australian army-issued suppressed Browning H-P in his right hand, his wide-brimmed bush hat on the floor, and a satisfied smirk on his flushed, round face.

'Where's the bitch?' he demanded.

Vaux nodded to the gilt-bordered doors of her bedroom. 'Don't kill her,' he said, fearing the Aussie's rage. 'We need to talk to her.'

Dawson moved to the bedroom door and knocked hard twice.

No answer.

'I'll deal with it,' said Vaux.

'She's probably got a gun, too, sport. Tell her to come out, arms raised. Tell her we want to talk.'

'And then what? Are we taking her with us?'

'You bet,' said Dawson. 'With certain conditions.'

'What are they?'

'She'll walk out with us, quiet as a cat, till we tell the bitch what to do. Okay with that, sport?'

Vaux moved to the door. 'Alena! Are you there? Let me in, please.'

There was no answer. Dawson tested the door. Firmly locked. He pondered for a few seconds, looked at Vaux, and then kicked the door with as much strength as he could muster. Now a splitting sound as the mahogany door crashed open into the dimly lit en suite bedroom. Dawson swung his Webley around to cover the room. But there was no target. Alena must have fled through the open french windows that opened onto a narrow balcony.

They both cautiously moved to the window and looked onto the balcony. She wasn't there. They looked down to see if she had jumped. But the traffic in front of the hotel continued to move at a sluggish, normal pace. A sedate liveried doorman was opening the door of an arriving taxi.

They turned back to the elegant bedroom. The walls were covered in dark blue silk, the furniture distinctly Louis Quinze, the bed unmade, a tangle of dark blue sheets. Dawson went over to the doors that led to the external corridor. They were ajar.

'The bird's flown, sport,' said Dawson.

They went back to the main room. A big-screen television above the small cocktail bar displayed a silent scene: Channel M, whose regular newsreader, the beautiful and elegant Melissa Theuriau, was mutely delivering the evening's political news.

Vaux said, 'Better go, Gerry. We need to think.'

'Hang on a minute, sport.'

He moved towards an elegant silk-covered chaise-longue, on which sat a discarded *Galleries Lafayette* plastic shopping bag. Then he went over to the bar where several sinister tools had been carelessly placed. He recognised some of the instruments: a syringe, a stunner, a hacksaw, a pair of surgical scissors, two walkie-talkies, a signal jammer, and a box of folded trash bags. He stuffed them into the shopping bag.

Vaux had left to use the gold-plated bathroom.

In a dark, Antipodean accent, Dawson muttered, 'The bastards planned to kill him in the bath, cut him up into body parts, walk out with him in a garbage bag, nobody any the wiser.'

Chapter 19

'What do you mean, he's MIA?' Craw snapped as he pushed himself up on his pillow.

It was 7 a.m. on Sunday morning, and he was still trying to sleep off the effects of too many vodka martinis the prior evening. He had gripped the encrypted office cell phone and held it tightly to his ear as he anticipated the reply a panicky Thursfield would deliver.

'Missing in action, sir. Disappeared. Never came home to his digs last night—unprecedented.'

'Really, Thursfield. Use some imagination. It's the weekend. He could easily have met a floozy or two in some sordid bar and gone back to her place. It wouldn't be the first time, for God's sake.'

'I'll keep monitoring his flat. That's all I can do, sir. Thought I'd better raise the alarm, as is my duty.'

'Yes, well, you did right to inform me. But it's Sunday, so we'll give the man a little leeway. Call me around eleven. I'll probably be up and about by then.'

Craw tried to snooze a little more. But the seeds of a possible fiasco had been effectively planted. He thought, *Let's say Vaux has done a bunk. We know he met and talked in plain sight to some Syrian official. And a watcher reported following him to the Syrian consulate on Rue Paradis, where he spent more than an hour. But that was it. There were no signs that he was preparing to do a bunk—get out while the going was good.*

No, Craw convinced himself that Vaux was simply acting true to form. Probably got drunk at the Bar du Port and at closing time went home with that semi-hooker Dominique. He had to admit, though, she was a knockout. Not that in his position he could or even wanted to test the waters.

He fell back to sleep for another two hours, woken by a slight tap at the double doors that signaled the arrival of his pre-ordered breakfast of French bacon and *omelet aux champignons*.

Meanwhile, Thursfield continued to look at the monitoring screen that spanned the cramped space of Vaux's safe flat. He felt the need to go down the one flight of stairs to the room itself; maybe the physical appearance of the place, the absence of his clothes, his habitual leather holdall, would reinforce his suspicion that Vaux had fled. On the other hand, an old pro like Vaux would hardly make an abrupt evacuation too obvious.

* * *

In Paris, for Vaux, it was the morning after the night before. Perhaps it was the shock of what happened after the pleasant, friendly dinner with Alena—the trap she had obviously set, the fatal outcome she and her co-conspirators had planned. But he could only recall a few of the events that followed Dawson's sudden, violent intervention.

He remembered Dawson pulling on his arm towards the emergency exit in the hotel corridor, trundling down the concrete steps three or four floors, then emerging in a plush carpeted corridor and crashing into a gilded, mirrored elevator just as the doors were closing. A tall, suave man in a dinner jacket and his elegantly gowned companion looked on with obvious disdain as Gerry, breathing heavily and supporting Vaux with a large arm around his shoulders, pushed his sausage-sized finger on the ground floor button. Then he vaguely remembered being bundled into the back of a Grand Cherokee and falling asleep on the wide back seat, with Gerry and the unknown driver up front.

Now he was in a large, comfortable bed under a blue coverlet, looking up to a yellowed, plastered ceiling with corner friezes and a small, dusty crystal chandelier hanging from the centre. He heard faint birdsong and the occasional soft beep of a car's horn.

Suddenly, a hard rap at the door. 'Come in!' Vaux shouted. 'Entrée.'

Gerry Dawson, large as life, in a blue track suit and trainers, stood at the door, tray in his hands. 'Baguette with ham, old man. And a big bowl of cafe au lait.'

'Just what the doctor ordered,' Vaux said as he pushed himself up, head resting on the silk padded headboard.

Dawson grabbed an upright chair with a straw seat. Its thin legs wobbled under his weight, so he got up and sat on the side of the bed.

'I can't thank you enough, Gerry. For last night, I mean. But my first question is why the hell were you in Paris? You never told me of any plans to go there.'

'It was a spur of the moment thing. Besides, I have a lot of friends here. Including the lady who owns this villa.'

'Where are we?'

'In a small town south-east of Paris. Commuter territory. She's a dentist, an old friend of mine. Tomorrow, you'll hear a lot of comings and goings as her patients come in and out for their cleanings and fillings.'

'So this is your own private refuge, your personal safe house?'

'You could call it that. My advice is to lay low, sport. For a while, anyway. I'm going back to Marseille; we'll be in touch.'

'Wait a minute, Gerry. Come on, old boy. You have to tell me more than that. How come you were at the right place at the right time?'

'Let's say I've got a lot of fingers in a lot of pies. Okay, louse? When you write my bio, I'll tell you everything. Meanwhile, lie low, and I'll call you to keep you up to date. I've a hunch you're in trouble not only with the Syrians but with your own home team.'

'Alena started to tell me last night; something about a home-grown plot to frame me as a double agent working for the enemy. Now you're telling me the same thing. What's your evidence, for God's sake?'

A pause while Dawson got his thoughts together. 'Look, sport, did I show you last night what a friend is?'

'Of course, it goes without saying. You saved my life—even when I was dumb and incompetent enough to walk into an obvious trap. I suppose I had come to trust Alena. She's lost none of her guile. What an actress. But why would she do this?'

'Never mind motives. I can think of a few. The Syrians look at you as a traitor, a leaker, and ex-lover of one of their most esteemed secret agents. You've told me all the stories about the Damascus paper and your love affair with her in Cairo. Even if she had a soft spot for you, old mate, the bureaucracy certainly didn't. Your friend Kadri betrayed them, or so they thought, and back in Tangier, you may remember, you conspired with him to mislead Damascus about the loyalty of two of their senior diplomats. That little caper was hatched solely to further your mate Kadri's career. You were his friend and co-conspirator, as far as they were concerned. So now they use her to get to you and eliminate the scourge, once and for bloody all.'

'Nicely put.' Vaux sipped his coffee. 'So you think I should stay here. For how long?'

'I told you. Let me do a good old recce. I want to find out what exactly is going on with your lot. But I've a feeling they're up to no good too—as far as you're concerned. They may be just as keen to have your guts for garters as the bloody Syrians.'

* * *

Alan Craw's usually sacrosanct lazy Sunday had been shattered by Thursfield's report and confirmation that Michael Vaux had disappeared. According to a later, out-of-breath, on-location bulletin from Thursfield in the narrow alleyway outside the Bar du Port, Dominique had reported that she hadn't seen Vaux or Gerry for two days. Indeed, according to Dominique, Gerald Dawson was due home that afternoon from a short trip to Cannes.

Dominique added that Dawson had been fulfilling his function as chairman of an ex-pat club based in Cannes, which met every six months for mutual backup and general spiritual support. She said the small group of Aussies convened in the piano bar of the plush Hotel Martinez, just down the Boulevard de la Croisette from the snooty Carleton Hotel, where the English stay.

'Yes, well. A likely story. She's giving the blighter cover. Odds on that the two amigos are partying together in the flesh pots of Cannes or wherever. Perhaps we just have to be patient. After all, Vaux wasn't under orders to report his every move.'

Thursfield, who theoretically had been very close to Vaux —via his newly-acquired technical mastery of audio-video technology— detected a heavy dose of wishful thinking on the part of his boss. But he chose not to demur.

* * *

After Dawson left him, Vaux got up, searched for the bathroom, had a quick shower, and went back to his room to dress. His clean shirt and underwear lay in his leather holdall at the Hotel du Sud. Only too aware of his negligence and against everything they had drummed into him at that long-ago crash course at Portsmouth's spook school, he had also left his Sig Sauer wrapped in a t-shirt in the bag's zippered side pocket.

He knew he had to ignore Dawson's advice to stay put for a while, not least because he felt a pressing need to retrieve the gun. Then he would walk to the Gare de Lyon and jump on one of the frequent trains to Marseille and points south.

He clattered down two flights of uncarpeted stairs to land in a large Portuguese-tiled foyer. The appetizing smell of roasting meat led him down a narrow passage to the kitchen. Two middle-aged women, one stocky and the other slim, turned to him and greeted him in unison: 'Bonjour, monsieur.'

The slim lady, with greying blonde hair wrapped into a bun, and round wire-rimmed glasses perched at the tip of her aquiline nose, moved towards him, gripped his arm, and motioned that he should follow her. They went into a large reception room with double doors partitioning the dining section from the lounge.

'I am Madame Lebar, and I have known your friend Gerald for many years. Are you comfortable, and will you stay for lunch?'

Vaux would love to have stayed with this interesting woman. But more urgent and dire action had to be taken. Perhaps more than anything, he must clear up the small matter of Alena's assertion that his own people—Gower Street or Vauxhall Cross— had cooked up some scheme to falsely accuse him of treason. It could, of course, have been her crude way of luring him back to Damascus. But what really bothered him was Dawson's advice to lie low. Was he just suspicious, or did he know something?

'I appreciate your offer, Madame. But I'm afraid I must go. I am due in Marseille later today and I have no time to lose.'

Madame Lebar looked disappointed. 'But you have only just arrived, Monsieur. Do you have to go so soon?'

'I will return soon to thank you properly for your hospitality, Madame. I shall come with Gerald and with ample notice next time.'

They both laughed, and Madame Lebar looked lost for words. 'It's just that on Sundays, of course, I have no appointments, and we would have had a lovely lunch and perhaps later, despite my faulty English, talk and set the world to rights.'

'Your English is excellent. But we'll talk and put the world to rights when we next meet.' Vaux knew the likelihood of their meeting again was practically nil. But he would remember her kindness if ever he needed a quick and safe retreat.

Vaux asked her if he could call a local taxi company to pick him up and take him back to Paris.

'*Mais, non*! There is a train every forty minutes direct to Paris, the Gare de Lyon. Much cheaper, non? The station is a ten-minute walk only. You turn right when you leave the house and then walk down a steep hill to *la gare*.'

Chapter 20

At Vauxhall Cross, MI6's headquarters on the south bank of the turbid Thames, Bill Oxley, the veteran spy catcher, had just heard, via his new and cheeky probationer-assistant, that a top priority message from Damascus had been received by the signals wallahs and would be in his hands 'momentarily,' once they decrypted it.

Oxley, who had noticed the young man's propensity to dart frenetically in and out of his windowless office like a jack-in-the-box, called him back before he could shut the sturdy, grey door.

'Yes, sir. Did you need something?'

'Yes, as a matter of fact, I do, Beaton. I would like to know whether you have ever spent any time in the States.'

'No sir, not that I know of. I mean, sorry, no, I have not.'

'Um. So where did the word "momentarily" come from—it's not commonly used in these fair isles of ours, is it?'

'Well, I suppose it means "in a moment," really. I guess I may have picked the word up from Hollywood films, or maybe from American novels.'

'There you go again. You use the word "guess" where the English idiom would be "suppose"—as in "I suppose I may have ..."'

'Never thought of that, sir.'

'All right. Let me have the decrypt as soon as they send it up.'

'Yes, sir.'

Oxley smiled to himself. It was easy to tease this younger generation. And Harold Beaton was right—US domination of the cinematic and literary arts probably did promote American English. But he was convinced of one thing: The decline and fall of England, perhaps exemplified by the surrender of its noble language to the American cousins, was clearly exacerbated by the traumatic spy scandals of the twentieth century [Maclean, Philby & Co.] as well as those that had occurred on his own watch.

He was jolted from these gloomy ruminations by the sudden reappearance of Beaton, who rushed in without his usual polite warning knock, a flimsy piece of paper in his hand. Oxley grabbed it and read:

TOP PRIORITY:

TO: PIERRE
FROM: DAMASCENE

DST CONTACT INFORMS OF PLOT TO ELIMINATE UNIDENTIFIED AGENT IN MARSEILLE. AGENT ON SPECIAL ASSIGNMENT. KNOWN TO ASSAD REGIME AS EX-ASSOCIATE AND CO-CONSPIRATOR WITH LATE AHMED KADRI. ROVING HUSSY TO BE LURE.

REGARDS

Oxley read and reread the puzzling message.

'Find out who the hell this HUSSY is, will you? The code boys may have worked it out.'

'Yes, sir. I presume, as your assistant, I am to be told who this equally mysterious Damascene is?'

'Cryptonym for our agent who works in the bowels of Syria's DST headquarters. A very noble man.'

'A double agent, I take it, sir.'

'Yes, of course—successor to a very great lady by the name of Tahiyya al-Sharqawi, late daughter of a former Syrian ambassador to the UK, and a senior analyst at the Damascus GSD headquarters.'

Beaton's jaw had dropped just perceptibly.

'Now go to it and see if we can't find out the identity of HUSSY.'

Oxley then picked up the secure phone and punched in Alan Craw's number. The receiver was picked up, but the line remained silent.

'Craw? It's the man from across the Thames.' This was a previously agreed extra security code for mutual recognition.

'Lovely here on the Riviera,' replied Craw, who used the prearranged reply.

'I've had a pretty shocking piece of news. Just in from our man in Damascus. Top secret. There's apparently a plot to eliminate one of our agents in Marseille. It can only be Westropp. The plan involves the use of some female to lure him into a death trap.'

Craw wavered. Should he inform Oxley of Vaux's sudden disappearance? Was he already dead? This bleak piece of news changed everything. But he had to bide time. There were too many ramifications. If the Syrians were plotting to kill Vaux, the very raison d'être of Operation Mascara was null and void.

He knew the Israelis didn't give a cuss if Vaux was dead or alive. They just wanted MI6 to terminate his services, once and for all. But the Syrians? Vaux had approached the Syrians himself. He had been seen talking with their man in Marseille at a restaurant in the harbour and later walking nonchalantly into their consulate on Rue Paradis.

'Yes, well, let me get back to you, old boy. Things seem to be moving fast. I think we should bring him home within a day or so.

My CPU operatives are getting bored, anyway. A few nights on the town, and they want to get back to Blighty and their better halves. So goes it. I'll be in touch soonest.'

Oxley, known throughout the Secret Intelligence Service for his uncanny intuition, sensed a brush-off, an evasive ploy. Craw was keeping something from him.

'Don't hang up. I'm anxious to know the latest news, obviously. What exactly has our mouse been up to these days before the cat pounces, as it were?'

Craw's excuses came easily. 'Oh, the usual thing. Late-night bars, drinks with the street girls. Thursfield says he's reading a lot. The classics, Forster and all that.'

'Um. Well, say hello to Thursfield for me. Oh, and ask him to get in touch soonest.' Craw heard the sudden click as Oxley hung up.

Craw, of course, decided to do no such thing. But he would take a Sunday stroll to that noisy and noisome Arab area where the safe house was located. Anyway, he was curious to know what Thursfield was up to in the sudden absence of Vaux. With Vaux disappearing into thin air, what was there for Thursfield to listen to and monitor?

* * *

At that very moment, Patrick Thursfield was fitfully rousing himself from a deep slumber brought on by a late Saturday night spent with a few new friends and fellow rugby fans at the Queen Victoria, an ersatz English pub in the heart of Marseille.

He had flashes of memory: the big television screen, New Zealand thrashing England, and the pub exploding in uproarious celebration. But then he fell back to sleep at the thought of another dreary day ahead. Since Vaux's disappearance, he had sat in the midst of his sophisticated video equipment with nothing to do except listen to the silence emanating from hidden microphones and gaze at screens that constantly scanned the static, shabby, uninhabited safe flat.

He was jolted by the sudden shrill ringtone of his secure mobile that sat on the floor beside his narrow bed.

'Yes?'

'Thursfield? Craw here. I'm coming round. Be there in fifteen minutes. We have a lot to talk about.'

'Yes, sir.' Thursfield got up, stretched his arms above his broad shoulders, and made for the narrow, plastic-curtained shower stall.

He was luxuriating in the cleansing warmth of the shower and the strong olive scent of the local Marseille soap he had developed a liking for, when the smartphone rang again, imperiously demanding his attention. He brushed the shower curtain aside and headed for his bed.

'Yes?'

'Craw again, old boy. Be downstairs when I get there. I've mislaid the keys.'

'Right, sir,' said Thursfield. He pressed the off button and muttered, 'Anything you say, sir.'

He vigorously toweled himself in front of the antique wormholed floor mirror Dawson had thoughtfully installed some years back. He observed a slight thickening around his usually narrow waist and hips. He resolved to resume the running regime he had abandoned since leaving the leafy suburbs of Chalk Farm, once Operation Mascara had come to its inevitably successful conclusion.

It was Sunday, so he slid into a pair of blue jeans and a matelot T-shirt he had picked up in a boutique on the busy Canebiere, the wide shopping street that led off from the Vieux Port.

Ten minutes later, he was standing in the centre of the safe flat, flipping through the paperbacks on Vaux's bedside table. He was wondering to himself why a man who, according to current hearsay, enjoyed such a close affinity with all things Arabic and the Middle East was so keen on classic English authors like Forster,

Spender, and Greene. Then he heard two hard knocks on the door, followed by three gentle taps. Craw had remembered the confidential knocking code.

'Hello, old man,' said Craw. 'The door downstairs was unlocked, so I just came up. Don't you lock up at night?'

'A cleaner comes in to do the stairs and floors, and I guess she forgot to lock the door when she left,' said Thursfield.

Craw smelled a rat. 'Even on Sundays?'

'Yes, she seems to come in and out at all times.'

'Bad security. We'll have to look into that.'

'Yes, sir.'

Craw was wearing a white linen suit, a blue shirt, and a blue-and-white polka-dot cravat. He headed straight for the worn, stained overstuffed armchair where Vaux, when in residence, sat and did most of his reading.

'Keeping well?' he asked.

'Yes, sir, thank you,' said Thursfield.

'I won't beat about the bush. But we've got an emergency on our hands. First off, have you picked up anything on the man's smartphones?'

'You mean Vaux?'

'Of course; damn it, man, who else?'

'Not a birdie. Haven't seen or heard from him since late Friday, I think it was.'

'So you let him just sneak away like some silent nymph?'

'Nymph?'

'Spirit, whatever,' Craw said impatiently.

'That was hardly my remit, sir,' Thursfield objected. 'I've been stuck in the operations room upstairs. Twenty-four hours a day. That's been my job from day one.'

'Yes, yes, I know. I'm just trying to think of my best move. We've been thwarted by slippery Vaux, and I'm mad as hell. Forgive me.'

At that very moment, the two stressed men heard a strange scratching at the door. It was the ancient Yale lock. Then a firm drive home; the lock turned, and the door opened. It was Vaux, somewhat disheveled, but in his usual casual jacket and khaki chinos.

He threw his leather holdall on the bed, looked at both men, and feigned surprise at seeing old comrade Craw with Thursfield in his one-room safe house. He had guessed his sudden disappearance would spark some concern by the architects of Operation Mascara, but he had done his bit. He had uncovered the terrorist sleeper cell and to take a few days off was hardly unpredictable.

What happened to him in Paris, and why, could wait.

'Well, Mr. Craw. We meet again.'

Thursfield stood unsteadily at the entrance to the small kitchen.

Vaux went over to him and shook his hand. 'Nice to see you again,' he said.

Craw was shaken at the sudden appearance of his old nemesis. But he was determined to find out what game he was now playing. He assumed a cool air.

'Look here, Vaux, where the hell have you been? You surely know you have to report to us your whereabouts twenty-four hours a day. You can't just walk out on an operation this vital without telling us.'

Vaux took his jacket off and went through to the kitchenette. Craw sat down again, and Thursfield suddenly excused himself. 'I have to go. See you both later, I hope.'

On the way to the door, he winked quickly at Craw, who guessed he was planning to climb the narrow staircase one floor to gear up the audio-video paraphernalia.

Vaux came back with a glass of chilled Evian from the mini-fridge.

'I would appreciate a full report of your activities over the last forty-eight hours, Vaux,' Craw said imperiously. He had put on a pair of wire-framed glasses Vaux had never seen him wear before. Craw had produced a small diary, over which hovered a slim, gold ballpoint pen.

'Really, old man. Nothing to make notes about. Went up to Paris for the weekend. The operation's over; surely I'm entitled to a few days' leave.'

'Where did you stay, and who did you stay with?'

'That's not your business, Alan.'

'You have not been dismissed from Operation Mascara,' Craw said. 'There are a lot of loose ends to tie up. I thought you would have guessed that.'

'What more do you want to know? I pinpointed the sleeper cell and assume arrests were made. Job done.'

'It's never that simple, Vaux. You should know that after all your years of clandestine operations. Who did you see in Paris, anyway? You owe us an account of your activities until we decide to terminate you.'

'That sounds ominous,' said Vaux.

'End your employment, then. Contract over and done with. Does that sound better?'

Vaux sighed. He wanted the pompous Craw out of there. Then to plan his encounter with Monsieur Bruno Valayer, the Syrian honorary consul who had so efficiently organised the rendezvous with Alena. Was he a co-conspirator in the attempt on his life?

Craw's long fingers drummed impatiently on his thin thigh. He was thinking of his next move in this disquieting development. Vaux was behaving like a loose cannon. He had been observed and photographed talking to the Syrian representative in Marseille. He had surreptitiously decamped to Paris, where he probably met up with other Syrian officials.

For the moment, he had decided to ignore what Oxley had told him about Damascene's serious allegations. The top secret report was hardly credible and probably another ruse perpetrated by the cunning Syrians on virtuous, not perfidious, Albion. Craw had become a man who refused to have his faith shattered. There was enough accumulated evidence to bring Vaux in. It was time to call in the troops.

But he must not show his cards just yet.

'Yes, well, we all love Paris. Meet anyone there you knew? Old friends, colleagues?'

'Please, Alan. It was as I told you. A lone touristy trip. Over the years, Paris gets a grip on you. I just felt like seeing some old familiar sites again.'

Craw had had enough of the sociable chit-chat. He stood up and went to the door. Vaux had his back to him, hanging shirts and a jacket in the small armoire.

Without a sociable word, he closed the door gently and quietly ascended the narrow staircase to Thursfield's operations room. From there, he called Warrant Officer Winslow, who was whiling away his time at the Holiday Inn Express, close to the St. Charles Station, along with his two colleagues assigned to apprehend Vaux once enough evidence had accumulated to charge him with treason. There was no time like the present.

Chapter 21

Mishka Arenson shrugged his shoulders and adopted a benign air of puzzlement at the verbal onslaught delivered by Andre Sagan, chief investigator [Paris] at the *Directorate General de Securite External* [DGSE]. Mishka had been called to the drab offices of France's spy agency in the twentieth arrondissement to explain the brutal assassinations of two Syrian nationals, suspected of being in the employ of the GSD, Syria's intelligence agency.

'I simply don't know why you should ask me these questions, Andre. It's a terrible crime, but what makes you think we have anything to do with this outrage?'

'Don't come all that innocence; butter wouldn't melt stuff with me, Arenson. It has all the familiar marks. My mind goes back to the Vendome killings. Remember? An Israeli outfit called the White Circle, with their expensive, plush offices in the Place Vendome, organised the assassination of one Al-Mabhouh, whom the Israelis claimed was a key member of the Palestinian Liberation Organization.'

'We denied all knowledge of that operation,' Mishka said calmly. 'Besides, White Circle is a private intelligence organisation usually involved in industrial espionage cases. Nothing to do with us.'

'Of course you deny everything, *mon ami*. Whoever's really behind the White Circle, they are known to specialise in wet jobs perpetrated against Arab politicians and activists. Then the case goes upstairs to our politicians, and all is forgotten. But we working stiffs are given the task of cleaning up the mess.'

Mishka, who had no idea why Sagan and his team should assume the Israelis carried out the brutal attack at the five-star Hotel Westin on the Rue Castiglione, shook his head slowly and appeared hurt by the assertions. 'I can only tell you, Andre, that I am quite certain, having spoken to the relevant people in the know, that you are barking up the wrong tree entirely.'

'But you surely do not deny that some sort of joint operation is going on between your people and the Brits. Our Marseille office has reported through wiretaps and field observations that you are collaborating with British security on some project about which you have not chosen to inform us.

'Non! The last thing you think of when one of your schemes is under way is to apprise the host country of your activities. And that, may I suggest, is because they are illegal at worst, politically unpalatable to us at best. Do you deny this too?'

Sagan started to twirl his George Clemenceau moustache, a sign of impatience. He reached over his desk to grab a blue packet of Gauloise and shook out a cigarette. He then fished out of his jacket pocket a silver Ronson, lit the cigarette, inhaled deeply, and blew out two provocative plumes of greyish black smoke towards his old friend.

Mishka waved his hand to disperse the spreading tobacco cloud. He saw Sagan's defiant gesture as a timely opening to conclude the awkward and embarrassing interview. 'Andre, my friend. We are allies. All of us are working together for the same goals, *n'est-ce pas*? So yes, there is a small combined ops taking place in the confines of the city of Marseille.

'But it is a very small affair and actually involves our cooperation in bringing a renegade Brit to heel. It involves the double-dealing of one of their long-time assets, and since the individual's treasonous activities have adversely affected the interests of Israel, we offered our support in the field. That's all. The Brits thought, quite rightly, that our cooperation could speed things up for them, and I can tell you now that I think the whole episode has concluded successfully. Otherwise, I wouldn't be taking a few days off in your great City of Light.'

'*Ah oui, bien sur*—sure, sure,' Sagan said, his hands in the air in total surrender.

At the door, Mishka asked in a low, conciliatory voice if Sagan's people had checked who had booked the room in which the two Syrian nationals were shot dead.

'A man by the name of Chaban. Name mean anything to you?'

Mishka shrugged a Gallic shrug and left.

* * *

In the cobbled sweep of the crescent-shaped building that housed the DGSE's nondescript command centre, Mustafa sat in the driver's seat of a rented Citroen C1, listening to an emotional Mohammed Abdu cassette. He was transported to his native country and knew he would exchange the elegance of Paris for the torrid heat and poverty of his homeland any day. His reveries were ended by a sudden rapping on the back window.

Mishka ordered him to drive south to the Place de la Republique and drop him at a small restaurant on the Rue Fauburg du Temple, which ran east of the big square to the Canal St. Martin area. And while he navigated carefully to enter the flow of traffic, would he please turn off that Arabic cacophony.

'Bien sur, monsieur. Nous allons a la Place Republique, tout de suite.'

Mishka leaned back in the plush comfort of the back seat. He thought his meeting with Sagan had gone well. Nothing had been resolved, the local gendarmes had made no progress as to the identity of the victims, and whoever shot them remained a mystery. Now he was about to find out whether his suspicions were justified.

The Bar du Theatre, so-called because it is located opposite a small variety playhouse on the Rue du Fauburg du Temple, is patronized mainly by cash-poor students, trendy millennials, and venturesome migrants from Algeria and the Mideast who liked to live in close proximity to the centre of major demonstrations and national protests on the nearby Place Republique [Note 9].

Fahmi, the Algerian owner of the Bar du Theatre, is a short, tubby man whose smile never leaves his face, perhaps because the money-spinning café-bar is busy from early morning until well after midnight.

Mishka hauled himself out of the car in front of the theatre. Mustafa drove off towards the canal area, where he would park until summoned on his cell phone. Mishka crossed the narrow street, saw that all the tables on the sidewalk terrace were taken, and dived into the dark gloom of the small bar and dining room.

He saw Yasin Ahmad with his back to the wall opposite the bar. He was drinking from a bottle of Heineken and waved languidly on seeing Mishka stride in like a young man in a hurry.

Mishka ordered the same as his friend as he passed Fahmi, who stood behind the bar and gave a smiling nod to welcome the vaguely familiar face.

Mishka sat down opposite his trusty Syrian cut-out, who remained seated on a worn and scratched red leather banquette.

'What have you got for me?' Mishka asked as he looked around the room for possible listeners. But it was well past noon, and there was only a couple at one of the other tables and a youth sitting on a high stool at the bar.

Yasin pushed his arm towards Mishka and opened his lined, tobacco-stained palm, like a lotus leaf seeking the sun: the time-honoured code for cash.

'Two of our subcontractors. I never knew them. But they do wet jobs. They do it before—no problems. Many times. But this time, they taken off-guard.'

Mishka sighed. 'Has the DGSE contacted your people?'

'No. Anyway, we would deny all knowledge.'

'There's going to be a big investigation. Make sure my people are not brought into it. Nothing to do with us, anyway.'

'But Mr. Mishka, you knew of the woman's involvement, didn't you? The woman from Damascus. She was there in the hotel.'

'What woman? I know nothing, Yasin. Nothing.'

Mishka looked around the bar and outside to the busy terrace. The mild afternoon had brought out the thirsty unemployed students. He fished out a bundle of euros.

Yasin exposed his grimy palm again.

Mishka said, 'Two thousand—a bonus for your good work. Keep the faith.'

Mishka then called Mustafa on the cell phone. He stood up and walked sedately to the street. The black Citroen sidled up, he clambered in, and fell into a deep sleep in the middle of the rush-hour traffic jam that now paralysed the storied Place Republique.

Chapter 22

In the tense atmosphere at the safe house on the Rue de Refuge, a livid Craw had quietly decided to act with decisiveness. Desultory conversation with Vaux had only made him more irritated and determined to launch his self-named Operation Homeward Bound without further delay.

On the third floor, Thursfield's eyes had been glued to the video screen. He was watching Vaux sort out his clothing; on the hidden camera that covered the entrance to the flat, he had observed Craw stealthily remove himself from the scene. Thirty seconds later came the coded knock on his door.

Craw tiptoed into the operations room. He did not want to distract Thursfield from his monitoring tasks. But his colleague took off the headset and pointed to the small screen: Vaux had now collapsed on the small single bed. They both heard a gentle, regular snore as the bolshie secret agent caught up with his sleep.

Craw sat down on the threadbare couch that Thursfield used as his bed. 'Listen carefully. I am about to order the CPU squad to commence operations. They will be here at 5 p.m. precisely. It will be quite civilised. They will knock on Vaux's door, gain entry into the safe flat, and arrest him forthwith—after reading the riot act or whatever they call the obligatory warning about anything he says may be used in evidence. You know what I mean.'

'Yes, sir,' Thursfield said, wide-eyed and trying to interpret this radical turn of events.

Craw paused to see if Thursfield had some constructive comment to contribute. But the MI6 probationer searched for words to hide his shock at Craw's sudden decision to wind up Operation Mascara. Something, he figured, must have happened in Paris that he didn't know about and Craw was keeping to himself.

'So that's about it, Thursfield. Mission accomplished. I will make sure you get a lot of the credit. You've done a good job, and it's taken a lot of patience and dedication on your part.'

'Thank you, sir. I assume then that my duties are more or less over and done with. I can dismantle this operations room and return to the UK with the Military Police team.'

'You'll do no such thing. I'm arranging their flight right now with British Airways. I've reserved the two back rows of the plane under government priority. They'll be more or less isolated from the other passengers in the back row, with Vaux in handcuffs in the middle seat. At least that's what I want to arrange. What do you say?'

'I'm sure British Airways will oblige,' said Thursfield.

'I want you to stay put. Your electronic gear will need some careful packing, no doubt. And we need all those audio and videotapes you have covering Vaux's stay in that bloody flat.'

'Yes, sir. But truth to tell, there's not much evidence that you could call incriminating.'

'Never mind about that. Vaux, like all double agents, has been very careful about anything that might be cause for suspicions. Just make sure you preserve every tape and record that pertains to his activities since he's been here in Marseille. They will all have to be meticulously analysed.'

'Yes,' said Thursfield. Then he checked the video feed and saw Vaux still prostate on the narrow bed, sleeping the sleep of the innocent.

* * *

Months later, in the dusty, dim watering holes of Westminster, and across the river on the south bank, the men and women who work in the shadier areas of public service were heard to opine quietly that at this critical juncture of Operation Mascara, the fast-spinning wheels went off the rails for the most mundane and trivial of reasons: like everyman the world over, Craw, the head of operations, had simply and forgivably lost his keys.

When Alan Craw got back to his hotel, he poured himself a stiff gin and tonic from the minibar. So now his big task was virtually finished. An indisputable success for all his peers and seniors to see. Next stop: the directorship of Department B3, once Sir Nigel Adair fulfills his promise to retire within the year. Then on automatic pilot to the cherished knighthood: *Sir* Alan Craw. In a solitary toast to his success, he downed the stiff g&t in one gulp.

He fished the BlackBerry out of his jacket pocket and dialed the Holiday Inn Express. He hoped Warrant Officer Winslow was not gallivanting around the harbour with his two minions. The hotel operator asked him to hold while she rang his room. No answer. She came back on to say she would try the bar. An ominous sign, thought Craw. It was early afternoon, and he wanted the head of his exfiltration team to be as sober as a judge.

'Winslow.' The voice was impatient and gruff.

'Thank God I've got hold of you, Officer. It's the green light. We have no time to lose. I want you to get over to the safe flat with your two colleagues and arrest the man Westropp as soon as possible. You will need to keep him in custody and get him to the airport, where I will meet you, and we'll go from there. I'm trying to reserve seats on the last flight out to Heathrow.

'At no time, I repeat no time, will you let Westropp out of your control. He has to be handcuffed as soon as you arrest him. Whether you read him the usual caution about saying anything on arrest is up to you. Over.'

Silence on the other end of the line. Craw heard ice cubes tinkle as Winslow finished off his rye and ginger. 'Yes, sir. Message received and understood. We are all here together at the small bar in the hotel's foyer. Will one hour from now be satisfactory? The arrest, I mean.'

'Yes, yes. But I've just had a thought. You'll have to come to me for the keys, won't you?'

'Nah. We have other methods of entry.'

'No, no. I don't want any violence or damage to the safe flat. It would arouse suspicions and encourage gossip. Just wait, and I'll recheck if I have the keys. Then you can burst in on him and have the advantage of surprise.'

'Very well, sir. One more thing: don't we have to have a warrant, sir?'

'Oh, God. Just take it as a given. I'll get London to issue an arrest warrant right now. Don't worry about such niceties, Officer. Let me take care of it. Hold on, please.'

Craw put the phone on the bed and went over to the big antique armoire, where a few suits were hanging. He searched every jacket and shook the few pairs of pants he had brought with him. He riffled the pockets of his brass-buttoned blue blazer as well as his seldom-worn leather bomber jacket.

The keys could not be found. Yet he knew he had seen them quite recently. He racked his memory and pulled out the drawers of the antique writing desk. He picked the phone up. 'Damn it; they've gone, disappeared. But I know what I have to do. I'll call you back in fifteen minutes. You should go to the safe house now. Wait outside the building till I arrive. I'd like Westropp in custody by late afternoon.'

Craw then checked the smartphone for Gerald Dawson's

confidential number. The hippie Aussie assigned to maintain the safe house on the Rue de Refuge was a reliable ally, he thought, loyal to the old country through thick and thin.

* * *

Dawson was shining glasses with a tattered tea towel and arranging them in neat triangular patterns behind the bar. He was listening with some nostalgia to a taped rendition of *Waltzing Matilda*, a gift from Dominique some years back. Australia's unofficial national anthem always sparked wistful memories. But he was jolted back to the here and now by vibrations emanating from what he called the 'Limey' phone tucked away in the back pocket of his frayed jeans. He quickly silenced the ghetto-blaster perched on the back bar.

'Yes,' he growled.

'Craw here, old boy.'

'Yes. I recognize your voice.'

'Good, good. There's a bit of an emergency, old boy. I need your keys to the flat on Rue de Refuge. I've lost my set, or else they've been stolen. I really can't say. I don't see why anyone would steal them. Anyway, could you get over to my hotel and give me your set? It's absolutely vital, a matter of national security. I'll be waiting for you in the lobby downstairs.'

Dawson poured himself a glass of soda water. He wanted to stall Craw while he thought about all the ramifications. It was Vaux's pad, as far as he was concerned. What had happened to change things? Did they want to search the place in his absence? Or had Vaux returned from Paris already, against his advice?

He came to a decision. 'Okay, sport. Give me about an hour. Do you want me to go there and open up for you, or would you prefer I bring the keys to your hotel?'

'I'd prefer you to keep out of this, please. It's a rather delicate situation. Just be here with the keys at my hotel within the hour.'

Dawson put the phone back in his pocket. He didn't like the sound of things. What the hell did namby-pamby Craw need Vaux's keys for?

At that moment, Dominique swept through the beaded curtain, plunked her big brown leather purse on the zinc bar, and headed for the kitchen. The click of her stiletto heels echoed around the empty bar.

'Look after the place for me for a couple hours, will yer?' he called out amiably.

He heard a loud clatter of dishes but no reply. Then he rushed outside and hailed a passing cab on the narrow, cobbled Rue de la Croix.

Chapter 23

Dawson threw a twenty-euro note at the driver and did not wait for the change. Despite Craw's oft-repeated edicts about the need for total security, the front door of the house was always unlocked for the various tradespeople such as locksmiths, electricians, and plumbers. Dawson climbed the uncarpeted stairs two at a time. On the first floor, there were three flats. At Vaux's door, he tapped the coded knock and then pushed the Yale key home.

Vaux was just rising from the bed. 'Gerry, my man. How are you?'

'Get dressed, mate,' Dawson said. 'We're leaving. And as you often say, there's no time to lose.'

'Jesus, I just got here.'

'Which you didn't listen to me, did you, sport? I told you to stay put with my friends in Montgeron till things quieted down.'

'Yes, but I had to do things here.'

'Never mind about that. Get dressed and pack your undies. We're getting out of here before Craw and his bloody henchmen take you away.'

'What on earth are you talking about?'

'Craw's riding in with the cavalry to take you back to London town, mate—by force, if necessary.'

Vaux threw some clothing into his half-unpacked leather holdall, slid into his khaki pants, and pulled on a soiled t-shirt. He slipped into his loafers and, preceded by Dawson, closed the door gently and skipped downstairs. The two men hurried across the street and hailed a cab.

Dawson's evacuation plan took the best part of four minutes. During which, unbeknown to himself or to Vaux, Thursfield, his dutiful watcher and keeper, had been enjoying a hot shower, luxuriating in olive-scented soap, totally oblivious to the fast evacuation of the man he was charged to keep under twenty-four-hour electronic surveillance.

As he toweled himself off, he walked over to the desk and flipped on the video. None of the four cameras showed the presence of a human body. There were four box screens on the monitor, and all represented still-life pictures of an empty flat. Thursfield zeroed in on the bed to make sure he was not mistaken. Then he looked at the screen that focused on the curtained shower. Was it possible that Vaux was hidden behind the yellowed plastic shower curtain? He saw no steam escaping from the narrow stall but resolved to wait a few minutes to make sure his suspicions were justified.

In a state of shock, he pulled on a pair of jeans and donned a blue-striped shirt, and headed downstairs to the safe flat.

* * *

Craw paced the spacious lobby of the Hotel Dieux, wondering why Dawson was taking so long to deliver a bunch of keys. He looked at his gold Cartier watch and regretted now that he hadn't told Dawson to meet him outside the Rue de Refuge safe house. After all, it was the centre of operations.

Then, through the spinning glass doors, he observed the habitually disheveled Outback man scrambling out of the back seat of a yellow taxi, looking more disorganised than ever. He slung a shabby leather Domke F-2 camera bag around his shoulder, a remnant from his days as a professional photojournalist.

Dawson was clutching the bunch of keys Craw had requested. 'Want me to come along?' he asked amiably.

Craw thought for a few seconds. No, he didn't. 'Quite all right,' he said. 'I'll manage. Just a routine check. Thanks all the same. And by the way, I think you had better get some duplicates made.'

* * *

About twenty minutes earlier, Dawson had brought Vaux to an apartment on the Canebiere, about five hundred yards east of the Vieux Port. It was on the fourth floor, and its sumptuous furnishings belied the external shabbiness of the building.

'You can stay here till this is all blown over, sport,' he had said after checking the adjoining rooms to make sure no one else was using the place. 'There's a brasserie downstairs. They can send food up if you want.'

In the taxi, Dawson had told him of Craw's request for the keys to the safe flat. He had been his usual blunt self. 'I smell a rat, mate. They're closing in—and you have to make up your mind how you're going to deal with this sorry situation you've got yourself into.'

Vaux had sat down on a white leather sofa while Dawson sorted through his spacious old camera bag.

'Look, Gerry. This is plain ridiculous. I was asked to do a job here. I did it. Case closed. I haven't done anything wrong. Even I am entitled to speak to an old girlfriend. So they saw me in Paris chatting with Alena. They put two and two together and made five. That's all.'

'Not as simple as that, if you ask me.'

Vaux looked at Dawson, who was still delving into the bag and pulling out an array of photographic equipment: zoom lenses, light sensors, a TTL strobe, a flash modifier, batteries, and memory cards.

'Got a new assignment?' asked Vaux.

'Nah, not really. After thirty years in the game, it's hard to give up. I used to be a Boy Scout, so I'm always prepared for something I can sell to the news boys. You never can tell.'

'Like the incident in Paris?'

Dawson emitted a sound between a chuckle and a snort.

Vaux then popped the question he had been wanting an answer to: 'Gerry, what were you doing in Paris? You saved my life, for heaven's sake. Don't you think it's about time you brought me into the loop?'

'Ever heard of ASIS?' [Note 10]

'That's a new one. No.'

'That's the problem with us Aussies. We don't brag enough. ASIS is our equivalent of your outfit. I know you're working for your intelligence people. Wasn't hard to work out, was it?'

'Tell me.'

'Some time ago now, a guy approached me at the bar of the press club here. He had a proposition. He wanted me to run a safe house for the Pommies, okay? So he got me to buy that old place on Rue de Refuge—all above board, in my name and all that. So now I'm host to various agents and cut-outs and contacts going through the city from wherever: North Africa, mostly. Algeria, Tunisia, Morocco. He paid me, too, just for looking after the place—arranging cleaning and all that, paying the mortgage. The bank manager thought I wanted it for a mistress; I should be so lucky.

'Then you appear out of the bloody blue. So I say to myself, Hang on; I'm going to follow this case for two reasons, mate. One, I consider you a friend and colleague, and I figure that somehow, and if form means anything, this guy is going to get into some sort of trouble, and I didn't want to find you floating in the old harbour with your throat slit.

'That's one. Two, my friends at ASIS supported me in my own little surveillance project, all right? I put a reliable watcher on you. For your protection, you understand. One recent morning, he informed me you're headed for the St. Charles Station, and you've bought a first-class ticket to Paris.

'Well, if that doesn't stir my curiosity, I don't know what will. So I rush to the station, get the next TGV to Paris, buy the ticket on the train. Meanwhile, I've asked the ASIS operatives in Paris to be quick and nimble, and find out where you're staying. We put the watchers on you; I sent them a shot of you I had taken some days before without you noticing. They saw you arrive at the Gare de Lyon that morning—and Bob's your uncle. I shadowed you with a helper that evening, and aren't you glad I bloody well did?'

Vaux shook his head. 'What a fool I am to have fallen for Alena's death trap.'

'I haven't finished. We happen to have a contact within the Syrian embassy in the posh seventh arrondissement, close to l'Ecole Militaire. Let's call him Monsieur X. So Monsieur X reports that this lady visits the embassy very seldom. But the two thugs I saved you from, Monsieur X identified as specialist hit men who did Assad's dirty work for him. When I say Assad, I mean their spy network, of course. Roving assassins, with a license to kill enemies of his regime, wherever they are.'

Vaux's thoughts were mangled by the loud clanking of two trams as they passed each other on the traffic-clogged Canebiere.

'Are you hinting that Alena probably had nothing to do with it?'

'I'm saying there's no sure evidence that she had a clue about what happened.'

'But how did she disappear so quickly?'

'Must have got into the other suite over the balcony and done a quick scarper. I checked later, and the next door apartment was unoccupied.'

* * *

The three undercover officers of the Close Protection Unit [CPU] of Britain's Royal Military Police drove slowly up the traffic-clogged Rue de Refuge in a rented Peugeot P4 jeep. Warrant Officer Winslow, the driver, manoeuvred into a tight parking space and turned first to Sergeant Kingston, who sat in the front passenger seat, and then to Corporal Smith, who was sprawled across the back seat on account of his long legs.

'Okay, men, action stations. We wait here for our chief to tell us what we are supposed to do. As I understand it, we are to enter the suspect's flat and arrest him calmly and peacefully. No violence will be tolerated. Should he resist, then you two will restrain him according to your training, but no excessive force.'

Corporal Smith raised his arm to indicate a question. 'Do we handcuff 'im, sir?'

'I've been thinking about that. But yes, I think that would be appropriate. Then you, Corporal, have the task to gather his clothes and any other belongings, put them in one of the trash bags we've brought along, and then await further orders.'

Sergeant Kingston took his Glock 17 from the holster and checked the chamber. Winslow looked with some disdain at the weapon.

'I don't think you'll need that, Kingston. This is a spy job. The chap could be armed, but I understand from the Whitehall gentleman that it's all very civilised when it comes to backroom spooks like these.'

The Whitehall gentleman suddenly emerged from the shadows. He had been waiting for the police contingent under a grocery shop's awning next to the safe house. He was wearing a wide-brimmed Panama hat. The afternoon sun, even in late September, was strong.

Craw ducked down and looked through the Jeep's open window to welcome his facilitators. 'Our suspect is up on the second floor, gentlemen. I have the keys, so there's no need to cause any disturbance on entry into the premises.'

He observed the team's tan and brown urban fatigues and wondered why he hadn't asked them to be less conspicuous and dress in civvies.

The four men ascended the worn wooden stairs to the second floor. Craw was about to knock but then changed his mind. He slid the Yale key home and quickly pushed the door open.

The three MPs stood well back, perhaps anticipating a fusillade of gunfire.

They saw Craw run into the room, throw the shower curtain open, disappear into the narrow kitchenette, and then reappear. A look of shock and bewilderment covered his face, and he flopped down into the shabby armchair to collect his thoughts.

Winslow nodded to his two men to stay put where they were on the landing.

'Looks like the bird has flown, sir,' he said in a sympathetic tone.

Craw was in shock and didn't answer. He suddenly got up. 'Stay here, Winslow, and tell your men to come in. They may find something in the mini-fridge.'

Winslow looked bewildered but signaled to Kingston and Smith to come into the flat.

Craw angrily marched out and climbed the next flight of stairs, two at a time. He knocked on the door of the operations room. He heard muffled noises, the scrape of a chair against the hardwood floor, and the clatter of china and glasses as they were put in some sort of order.

The door flew open. Thursfield, disheveled from his recent shower, wore a black silk dressing gown. Craw saw that his blue eyes were unusually glazed and that his arm was raised to prevent any spillage from the balloon glass in his hand. A large measure of some golden orange-amber liquid churned gently in the glass, and Craw, a connoisseur of brandies, recognized the sweet aroma of Courvoisier.

'What on earth's going on here, Thursfield?' he snapped as he stepped past his colleague into the cramped operations room.

'My morning aperitif, sir,' he said.

Craw detected a rebellious, bolshie attitude.

'Bit late for that, isn't it?'

Thursfield closed the door behind Craw, who now sat on the upright chair facing the complex array of video and audio equipment.

'I've failed in my duty, sir. Vaux seems to have fled the nest, and I missed it. He must have suddenly evacuated while I was in the shower an hour or so ago.'

Thursfield then sat down carefully on the edge of his bed.

'I know he's gone. His luggage too. I want to know why you've chosen this critical moment to get sloshed, that's all.'

'That bottle—I bought at Heathrow Duty Free. Never taken a sip until this morning. Want one?'

Craw realised the man was trying to drown his sense of failure. He was blaming himself for the fiasco. 'Far too early. And you should stop right now. Make some coffee for both of us. We have a lot to discuss.'

Chapter 24

In London, at about the same time that morning, Bill Oxley read and reread the decoded message he had received two days earlier from Damascene, MI6's asset who operated within the core of Bashar Assad's regime in Damascus. There was something that did not add up. As was his wont, he wrote a memorandum to himself:

> *Damascene claims a plot is under way to kill a British agent on special assignment in Marseille.*
>
> *Moreover, said British agent reportedly 'known to Assad regime as ex-associate of late Ahmed Kadri.'*
>
> *This points without doubt to Michael Vaux aka Derek Westropp. So far, so good.*
>
> *But then, the coded message reads: 'ROVING HUSSY TO BE LURE.'*

RESEARCH ON CODE NAME 'HUSSY' still under way.

'ROVING' may indicate mobile or travelling agent.

Just writing the known facts of the case sometimes helped Oxley fill in the blanks. But he was still flummoxed.

He picked up the internal phone. 'Beaton. Come in here, will you?'

Beaton quickly appeared in front of his boss. 'Yes, sir, what can I help you with?'

'Any development on the search for HUSSY?'

'No, sir. Bradford's people on the Mideast desk haven't responded yet.'

'I see; thank you. You may go.'

As Beaton turned to the door, Oxley regretted his rather cold attitude towards the probationer. 'Wait a second. I'm just wondering how we can expedite the process. We're dealing with life and death here, at least according to our agent in Damascus.'

Beaton did not answer.

'I think we should think outside the box, if you know what I mean.'

'Explore new avenues of possibilities, sir?'

'More or less, yes. I want you to carefully study our files on this character Vaux, whom we suspect of long-time double-dealing with our Arab foes. That's what Operation Mascara is all about. I've a feeling HUSSY, who is presumably going to lure the man into a trap, is known to him and could even be an old lover. Hence the "lure" bit.'

'Yes, sir.'

Beaton turned around to leave.

'Beaton, where do you intend to start your research?'

'Registry, sir.'

'Good thinking. Go to it.'

Oxley looked down at his self-written memo. 'HUSSY—what a damn silly code name.' Then his office landline gave out a low-key ring.

'Oxley.'

'Bradford here.'

Doug Bradford had been head of Vauxhall's Mideast and North African desk for about two years. The two men only knew each other from occasional crisis meetings and their joint appearances at ad hoc committees called to deal with sudden, unforeseen emergencies. They had never consulted one another on Operation Mascara for the simple reason that the enterprise had been created and run by Department B3, the independent group originally formed a decade or so ago. Department B3's purpose was then described, rather grandiloquently, thus: 'To spearhead rapid-response strategies to tackle immediate and short-term contingencies arising out of the volatile Middle East theatre.'

'Yes, Doug.'

'What's this business about HUSSY? I hear you and your colleagues are asking everyone on my desk to identify her.'

'Not at all, Doug.' Oxley decided he would not confirm his recent orders to Beaton.

'I met one of your men—Beaton, I think his name was—at the Black Dog the other night, that's all. Said he was working on the problem and wondered if I could help.' [Note 11].

'I'll have to speak to him. He's a probationer and a bit green, perhaps somewhat naïf. I abhor loose talk, and that pub's a sieve. Eavesdroppers all over the place. I saw a bloody Russian there the other night—a man I know for sure is a senior FSB officer at their London station.'

'I always sit in a corner booth and speak in low tones. The loud music helps,' said Bradford. 'Anyway, I think you should know that HUSSY is one: obviously female, and two: a very special source of information within Assad's rapidly decreasing circle of trusted confidantes. She works in tandem with Damascene, who succeeded the late, great Tahiyya al-Sharqawi. In short, she is a priceless asset.'

Later, Oxley told colleagues that he was gobsmacked on learning that HUSSY was on their side yet fingered as the lure to entrap Vaux. On the other hand, of course, HUSSY would be following B3's orders to please her masters. But who were her masters? Assad or Sir Nigel Adair, Craw, and company? The whole project was becoming extremely complex.

Oxley said quietly, 'I see. Then I'm a bit at a loss as to how to deal with this latest development. B3's team are up to their necks in an operation in Marseille to entrap one of their men long suspected of being too friendly to the Arab regimes—feeding them top secret info and all that. To ensnare him, they've concocted an elaborate scam. But now we're told that HUSSY is out to get this individual—in other words, eradicate one of their own team. It doesn't make any sense to me, Doug.'

Silence on the other end of the phone line suggested Bradford was also trying to think things through according to basic logic. After a long pause, he suggested they talk later.

The phone tinkled as soon as Oxley put the instrument back in its cradle.

'Oxley.'

'Bill! How are you?' It was Angela Morris, deputy chief of MI6's Special Operations division, more commonly called by staffers the 'dirty tricks team.' Oxley had taken her for a drink just after her brilliantly executed wiretapping and electronic surveillance operation at Michael Vaux's home in Hertfordshire back in September. He recognized her seductive, low-key voice.

'Angela, how are you?'

'I enjoyed that drink we had at your club. I wondered if I could reciprocate, maybe later this week.'

'That would be very nice. Leave it with me, will you? We're going through a bit of a crisis right now. And until I have some answers, I don't think I'm going to be very sociable.'

'Oh, dear, what can the matter be?' She sounded a tad sceptical.

'Remember your little operation in Hertfordshire?'

'Yes, of course. I trust it produced the desired results.'

'Well, that's the whole point. I don't think we ever told you the end result. We found nothing whatsoever incriminating or doubtful from the listening and video systems you installed. And that only adds to the puzzle I'm now facing. If you want to know the truth, I think Vaux may be totally innocent of the serious breaches in security that triggered your initial surveillance operation. It's a long story—and when the dust settles, I'll give you a complete report.'

Angela was shocked. 'So all of my team's talents, not to mention my private and supreme personal sacrifice, were all totally in vain?'

'Maybe, maybe not. I'm really not in a position to say.'

She seemed lost for words.

Oxley said, 'I'll let you know when this potential fiasco is finally concluded. Then we'll have that promised drink, Angela.'

Angela did not respond, so Oxley put the phone down.

* * *

Vaux had food sent up from the ground-floor brasserie. He drank two Kronenbergs, switched on the TV, and watched the evening news.

He loved Dawson for all his efforts and his advice to stay low and await developments. He trusted the Aussie with his life; after all, he did kill the two would-be assassins, and he was now chasing down all the leads that might solve the riddle of his attempted arrest by his own team.

But he was restless. He couldn't sit and do nothing while Dawson embarked on some complex investigation into a conspiracy by his own people to frame him and then arrest him for presumably traitorous acts.

An even darker thought: were the Paris thugs employed by his own side or by the Syrians? And what was Alena's involvement? Was she a co-conspirator in the attempt to kill him, or was she an innocent bystander?

There were too many unanswered questions.

The street was busy: Trams and taxis clogged the Canebiere, families and shoppers crammed the sidewalks, youths on raucous motor scooters weaved in and out of the traffic. He strode towards the harbour, a new burner in his hand, his Sig Sauer firmly in its underarm holster.

He found a solitary table at the back of a quayside café, sat down to face the entrance, and watched the evening parade pass by. He punched in the memorised numbers.

''otel Dieux, bon soir.' A young female voice, willing to help.

'Oui, Madame.' Vaux asked the operator in his best anglicized French if a Monsieur Craw was staying at the hotel.

After a pause, the receptionist came back to him. 'You want I put you through, Monsieur?'

'Non, non, Madame. I have to leave a package at the front desk. He is expecting it. If you could just give me the room number. The package will be left at the desk within half an hour.'

Another pause while an animated debate ensued among several front desk staff. They came to a Gallic compromise which resulted in the repetition of the receptionist's original suggestion.

'Monsieur Craw is in Suite 403. Would you like me to connect you?'

'Non, non, Madame. I am in a terrible rush. I will put the room number on the package and leave it with your people at the front desk, if this is satisfactory.'

'*Mais oui.* We will see it is delivered.'

Vaux said, '*Merci bien*, Madame.'

Ten minutes later, he finished his small espresso, reemerged on the crowded sidewalk, and walked purposefully to the imposing hotel, floodlit against the clear starry night. The hotel, a former civic hospital, stood at the peak of one of the hills that surround the Old Port. He walked up the steep steps that led to the front entrance and was out of breath by the time he reached the lobby. He sat down on a copious red leather armchair close to the concierge's imposing Louis XIV oak desk.

Vaux knew he had the advantage of surprise. He also guessed that the only companions likely to be with Craw would be harmless unarmed colleagues like Thursfield, or even Dawson, his fifth column ally. So he didn't expect any problems.

Above all else, he wanted to learn why Craw, backed by the mandarins at Vauxhall Cross, had decided to move against him so suddenly and unpredictably. It made no sense. The loaded Sig Sauer was an insurance against any attempted strong-arm tactics by Craw or anyone who happened to be with him.

Chapter 25

Sir Nigel Adair, head of Department B3, was proud of his nonconformist subsection's achievements over the past decade or so. And he knew that a significant contribution to his perpetually understaffed offshoot of MI6's Mideast and North Africa desk had been made by one Michael Vaux, aka Derek Westropp, a former journalist and restless retiree.

So he had never been happy with his deputy Alan Craw's enthusiastic drive, even perhaps obsession, to prove Vaux a long-time double agent in the service of Syria and pan-Arab interests. Sir Nigel remained unconvinced even as Craw collaborated with Bill Oxley, Vauxhall's renowned spy catcher, to ensnare Vaux in a fake plot hatched by fictitious Marseille-based Arab terrorists.

Both Oxley and Craw had assured Sir Nigel that Vaux, who would be appointed the key man in Operation Mascara, would be so closely monitored and shadowed that the evidence against him would quickly emerge. Vaux's detractors were convinced that he would expose his true loyalties by warning his Arab contacts that MI6 was on to them.

Sir Nigel sat at his oversized desk, rearranging various nostalgic objects like ancient inkwells, fountain pens, a silver cigarette lighter, a small box of rubber bands, and paper clips. They all had their appropriate time-honoured positions. He performed such operations whenever he was trying to suppress his good humour. By lifelong habit, he liked to project a serious, grave, and thoughtful image to his colleagues and minions.

But he couldn't deny that he was in a very good humour that morning. For he had just had a call from Doug Bradford, head of the Mideast and North African desk [what Sir Nigel always called 'Head Office']. The call had been made via the scrambled telephone line between Vauxhall Cross and Gower Street.

And what Bradford told him was what Sir Nigel's teenage granddaughter would call 'dynamite news.'

* * *

Vaux got up from the deep leather armchair, looked casually at the concierge as he strode to the elevator, and nodded as if he were a resident of the hotel. The concierge smiled, gave a reciprocal nod, and resumed his phone conversation.

Emerging on the fourth floor, Vaux looked at the direction plaque for Suite 403. He turned left and walked towards the end of the wide corridor. At the door, he listened. He heard the low mumblings of a TV. No voices, no conversation. He reckoned Craw was alone.

To forestall Craw from slamming the door on him and then calling for assistance, he pulled the Sig Sauer from the leather holster and checked the manual safety catch.

He knocked lightly and turned his back on the fisheye peephole. Then he heard the click, and the door opened.

As Vaux later related the storied encounter, Craw was

apparently alone and doing his Noel Coward number. He wore a blue silk dressing gown, a long-stemmed champagne glass in one hand, and a long antique cigarette holder in the other. A miasmic haze of pungent black tobacco pervaded the room.

'What the hell?' Craw exclaimed, retreating quickly from the mini-foyer to let Vaux enter the suite.

'Sorry about the gun, Craw, but I thought you might not let me in. Relax. I just want you and I to talk over a few things. Shall we?'

Craw disposed of his Sobranie Black Russian cigarette in a large ceramic ashtray. Both men stood confronting each other. Craw was damned if he would invite a traitor to sit down.

'What's this all about, Vaux?' he asked.

'That's a funny question the day after you had your goons try and arrest me.'

'Please respect our diligent military police.'

'Is that all you have to say? Don't you think you owe me some explanation for all that's happened? What have I done? I think I know what you *think* I've done. But I can tell you this: you and whoever else is in on this frame-up have a lot to answer for.'

Craw emitted a dismissive guffaw and sat down heavily in a red leather armchair. He adopted the posture of a thinker.

'Look, man, what's happening here is entirely the result of your own, well, predilections.'

'Predilections?' Vaux echoed scornfully.

'You've brought it upon yourself. All these years of divided loyalties. The great Arab cause. The Philby-type love affair with all things Arab. Philby's father, the late great Saint John B. Philby, suffered from the same obsession. He had a lifelong love affair with the Mideast and the Arabs. His son was perhaps the biggest traitor Britain had the bad luck to produce. But you're all the same, you Arab lovers.'

Vaux had never seen Craw so out of control. Spittle dripped from his mouth as he spat out his hatred. He was breathing heavily as he lapsed into silence.

Vaux, the Sig Sauer still in his hand, walked over to the tall windows. He could feel a slight chill in the air. The night sky was clear, and a sickle moon hovered over the harbour. There was nothing to say. So without looking at Craw, he walked across the big room, put the handgun back in its holster, and left the room, closing the door quietly behind him.

The door acted as a muffler, but he heard Craw shouting, 'Don't know what Anne would think about all this!'

* * *

Meanwhile, at Department B3's shabby offices in Gower Street, Sir Nigel prepared for the first-ever visit of Doug Bradford, the youngish head of the MI6's Mideast desk. Miss Spencer, who had temporarily filled the beautiful Anne's position as chief typist, office filer, and general dogsbody, fussed around his tidy desk and placed an ancient Windsor chair to face Sir Nigel as he watched her performance over his half-moon spectacles.

'As soon as he comes, send him in. Then just bring a couple of coffees in that Spode chinaware my wife donated to the office, will you?'

She nodded to acknowledge the request and left. Sir Nigel now yearned to light his pipe but knew he mustn't break the vow he had made to Lady Adair on New Year's Eve, nearly twelve months ago. He started to feel somewhat drowsy. The room was hot, and the sash windows had jammed since early summer. The portable air conditioner had given up the ghost on the final day of September's short heat wave.

A noise roused him. Doug Bradford, tall, thick-set, with thinning brown hair, walked in unannounced, threw his briefcase on to the floor, and slumped down on the Windsor. He gripped the wooden arms and said he was pleased to finally meet Department B3's head of operations. He stood up and reached over Sir Nigel's desk to shake hands.

'Yes, well. Of course, I usually liaise with Sir Percy, so our paths never seemed to cross, eh?'

'Quite right. Well, sir, I have some very good news for you—in the sense, that is, that I believe you only reluctantly gave the go-ahead to this abominable Operation Mascara. I understand, of course, that you have always been sceptical of its, shall we say, raison d'être?'

'Yes,' Sir Walter said. 'I understood from your brief message that the whole effort has been a waste of time, in that our man is completely innocent of the charges which form the whole justification for the bum steer—and the wanton indifference to taxpayers' money, I might add.'

'Yes, sir. Exactly.' Bradford then took out a slim, silver cigarette case, popped it open, and proffered a Gold Leaf as he leant forward over the desk.

'Good God, man, no. I'll be burnt at the stake when Lady Adair smells the stuff on my clothes. Can't touch anything like that. Sorry.'

'Do you mind if I smoke?' Bradford sounded rather diffident, and Sir Nigel liked that in a senior man of the SIS.

'Go ahead. But let's get down to the business at hand,' Sir Nigel said as he waited patiently for Bradford to light up with a cheap plastic lighter, close the silver case, and slide it in the inside pocket of his dark grey suit.

'Indeed, yes.' He opened the slim leather briefcase he had brought with him and took out one sheet of A4 paper. It was a brief note from Sir Percival Bolton, head of MI6.

Dear Nigel,

I want you to know definitively that the charges against your man WESTROPP are to be dropped forthwith and the so-called OPERATION MASCARA is to be wound up immediately.

Bradford, an excellent man with a sound record [a Knighthood is imminent] will explain—with the help of new London resident Alena Hussein!

Bottoms up!
Percy Bolton

Sir Nigel's draw dropped, just perceptively.

'Well, that's a turn-up for the book.' He took off his spectacles and looked over to Bradford, who had been watching Sir Nigel closely.

'There is someone I think you should meet, Sir Nigel. She's waiting patiently in the outer office.'

Sir Nigel's eyes widened and he made a gesture to indicate Bradford should bring in the mystery lady. Bradford went to open the door. The woman stood in the door frame like an actress waiting in the wings for her inevitable cue.

'Good morning, Sir Nigel,' Alena Hussein said softly.

Adair stood up—more in shock than any nod towards convention. 'My God! Alena, I never expected to see you again. What in the world is going on? Bradford—explain please. And do sit down, Alena.'

Bradford gestured to the chair where he had been sitting, then brought another spindly wooden upright from close to the sash window.

Sir Nigel put his arms on his desk and took a long look at the woman he had considered to be one of Britain's most ruthless enemy agents; for the last decade or so, she had successfully penetrated the secret corridors of power. Worse, her treachery was perpetrated with all its thoroughness under his watch. But here she was again, thought Sir Nigel, with her long, black hair, the Arabic slope of her nose, the sparkling deep brown eyes, and not an ounce heavier than when he last set eyes on her.

He chose to say nothing more.

Bradford took his cue. 'We are both sorry if this development shocks you, Sir Nigel. But perhaps you have to understand one thing perfectly clearly—'

'Get to the point, dear man, before I collapse in shock.'

'Yes, sir; well, it has to be said that Alena Hussein has been working for us, diligently and loyally, for the ten years or so since she quote "defected" to the Syrians. We won't bore you with history, but you will remember that she was reportedly killed in the attempt on Vaux's life at the Chixham military base. Vaux was holed up there with colleagues towards the end of Operation Saladin; two or three Syrian thugs wormed their way into the base, a firefight ensued, and among the alleged victims, besides the two gunmen, was the lady who now sits before you.'

Sir Nigel looked sceptical. 'I remember that tragedy. The terrorists tried to kill Vaux and his party, but everyone escaped through some sort of underground tunnel built to connect the old monastery on the grounds of the base with the small cottage they were staying in. The handful of goons was wiped out by our guards. Among the dead was a woman identified as Alena Hussein.' Sir Nigel looked mournfully at Alena, who also betrayed a frisson of sadness.

Alena took the opportunity to speak up. 'Sir Nigel, you must understand what really happened that early morning. I had been called back to London by my head of station, and to take my place, they sent a young lady, a probationer on the embassy staff. They lied to her and said it was just an exercise in hostage rescue, and she'd return to her normal duties after the mock raid at the army base.

'Meanwhile, I was quickly exfiltrated via Luton Airport to Paris and then by private jet back to Damascus. There I resumed my undercover duties for MI6.'

Sir Nigel said, 'Continue, Bradford. Fill me in.'

'What Alena states is 100 per cent accurate. She has been working for us all along. She has been responsible for priceless intelligence regarding Assad's war on his own people; she has filled us in on his occasional dastardly nerve gas attacks on civilians—including women and children. Above all else, she recently established a pipeline of invaluable intelligence on Russian military operations in Syria, thanks largely to a short-lived relationship with a key FSB agent operating out of the capital.'

Bradford turned to face Alena. 'Is that a reasonably accurate summation of your activities over the last year or two?'

'Absolutely. Though the bit about the "relationship" I might take issue with.'

Sir Nigel and Bradford both emitted a sympathetic titter.

Alena continued, 'But I also had access to our people within the GSD who were in close contact with the Turks. We informed them of various Kurdish maneuvers and ploys planned against Turkey's armed forces, who were interested in keeping the northern border with Syria intact.

'But, Sir Nigel, may I say that I was unaware that you had been kept out of the loop regarding my work for your country. It is most regrettable.'

Sir Nigel grunted. 'Without appearing too cynical, I assume all these claims by Alena have been checked out. Forgive me, Alena, but one must do one's due diligence.'

Bradford said, 'Yes indeed, sir. You can take it to the bank. Our trusty long-time agent, the late Tahiyya al-Sharqawi, aka "Gertrude," who operated at the heart of the Assad regime in Damascus, regarded Alena as one of her most reliable allies in their efforts against Assad's criminal conduct.'

Alena and Bradford exchanged mutually sympathetic smiles.

Bradford said, 'But now we come to the nitty-gritty. About eighteen months ago, Alena was in such good standing with her bosses at the GSD that they appointed her to the post of plenipotentiary—a sort of roving ambassador, investigator, or uber-agent. She was supposed to troubleshoot problems and mix-ups most intelligence outfits get into from time to time.

'When she heard about Operation Mascara in Marseille, she approached a Mossad contact she's known for years. He shall remain nameless. But the bottom line is that the whole operation was phony, a hoax, suggested by the Israelis and by certain members of our own service, to test the loyalty of one of your occasional hires—namely, Michael Vaux.

'Vaux had never been liked by Tel Aviv, a dislike stemming from his finger-pointing Mossad as the probable perpetrators of the targeted assassination of a Syrian nuclear scientist who had defected to the UK and was then under Vaux's care.

'Another black mark against Vaux, apparently, was a comment he made to his Syrian friend Ahmed Kadri while they stayed together at a villa in Tangier many moons ago; the remark was recorded without his knowledge.

'It was to the effect that Israel was the only country in history that had got away with grabbing another people's land and in sixty years had shown no signs of giving it up, nor any inclination to enter serious peace talks.'

Alena interrupted. 'I saw he was now in a lot of danger. Operation Mascara, as it was called, was a hoax. Our side, with Israeli collusion, had conceived a terrorist plot to blow up some mosque in Algiers in order to spark an uprising against Bouteflika and his ruling elite. It was pure fiction. Vaux's enemies, who all along figured he was a double agent for Syria—they've thought that since his escapades under Operation Helvetia—gambled that he'd lose no time in contacting his Syrian sources, who they presumed had a channel into the fictitious terrorist cell in Marseille.

'I wanted to forewarn him. I still have a soft spot for him, Sir Walter. I believe you are aware of that.'

Sir Nigel's eyelids flickered, and a rosy flush came to his cheeks. He just perceptively nodded in agreement.

The three-part conversation then became more general.

Sir Nigel was quite ecstatic to learn that Alena, whom he had welcomed aboard a decade or so ago, when she had walked in to offer her services to queen and country, was about to chalk up another coup—one that helped to finally quiet the persistent talk and doubts about the loyalty of Michael Vaux, whom he himself had recruited and was, in the final analysis, accountable for his subsequent acts.

After they shook hands, Sir Walter casually asked a natural question: 'And where will you be based now, my dear? I presume personnel, or Human Resources, as they call it these days, won't have the good sense to send you back here to Department B3.'

'I think that's to be decided within a few days,' said Bradford.

After the three engaged in a round of handshaking, Sir Nigel sat down heavily in his high-backed leather chair. He was not bewildered by the turn of events, he told himself. But he felt the beginnings of a tinge of resentment. Why had he not been in the loop? If Alena had been a double agent for the home team all along, why hadn't Vauxhall told him? Instead, they left him in the wilderness, thinking all those years that she had been a traitorous spy, an expert in deception and trickery, loyal to the Arabs, and working in their interests.

But Sir Nigel was resilient. The powers that be, he told himself, should not be questioned. They had their own reasons for keeping Alena's story and true allegiances to themselves. Even so, he resolved to speak in no uncertain terms to Sir Percival Bolton on their next lunch date. He would tell Sir Percy that under his stewardship, he had taken the firm to absurd and extreme lengths in the implementation of the 'need-to-know' mantra.

Chapter 26

As soon as Vaux had left, Craw called Warrant Officer Winslow at the bare-bones Holiday Inn Express, close to St. Charles Station in the centre of Marseille.

Winslow, who found his small room claustrophobic, sat at the tiny bar in the hotel's lobby, sipping a rum and Coke. He had changed from his army fatigues into a blue blazer with shiny brass buttons and the grey gabardine pants his wife had bought for what she called his 'Mediterranean escapade.'

He felt his phone vibrate in the inside pocket of the blazer, pulled it out, and hit the lighted incoming call panel. 'Winslow.'

'Craw here, old boy. Look, I know this afternoon was somewhat of a fiasco, but I don't think we should just sit on our asses and let our quarry get away to who-knows-where.'

'Yes, sir,' said Winslow, as he grabbed the old-fashioned to drain the last of the rum.

Craw continued, 'I know our man. He will be walking the streets, popping into small bars, maybe some of the bigger hotel bars. He'll be restless and reluctant to sit and hide in some small room out of sight. I know him well. Therefore, I want you to have your contingent patrol the streets of Marseille, particularly around the harbour area, the tourist hot spots where Vaux will think he's protected by the crowds of people. What do you say?'

'Well, sir. You are probably correct in your appreciation of the situation. But I must just caution you that this is a very big town, and we'd be looking for a needle in a haystack, wouldn't we.'

'Do you have an alternative plan, Winslow? You failed in the last operation—'

'Excuse me, sir. That was no fault of mine or my men. The culprit, if you want to call him that, had fled, done a disappearing act. Nothing we could do.'

'Quite. I understand that. But you can't just sit there as if you're all on some sort of compassionate leave, eh? No. Let's get out into the streets and chase down the man who has betrayed our country. It's a serious business, Winslow.'

'I'm aware of that, sir. We will do our best. I only have two men, remember, so don't expect miracles.' Winslow punched the off button.

* * *

Sir Nigel Adair, who had just wished Alena Hussein, aka Barbara Boyd, goodbye and good luck, asked Mary, the temp who had taken Anne's place, to get hold of his deputy in Marseille immediately.

'Yes, Sir Nigel?' Craw said, as smoothly as he could manage.

'I'm aborting Operation Mascara as of this minute,' Sir Nigel said with uncharacteristic authority. 'It's finished, wound up as of now—definitively. Do you understand? Pack your bags, and report to me soonest.'

'But sir. I don't understand. We are on the brink of bringing Vaux in. My MPs are at this very moment combing the streets of Marseille to waylay our traitor—'

'Traitor?' Sir Nigel snapped as blood rushed to his face. 'Damn it man, Vaux has been totally exonerated by the top brass over at Vauxhall. Get back here soonest, bring Thursfield with you, and leave Vaux be.'

'Yes, sir,' mumbled Craw, who in later renditions of his story told colleagues he had been stricken to the core of his being.

* * *

Six weeks later, the slow wheels of counter-intelligence began to turn: a three-man commission of inquiry, held behind closed doors within the bowels of the Thameside headquarters of the Secret Intelligence Service, confirmed the sad story of an aborted operation that should never have got off the ground.

The three judges, all internal staff members, charged that preparations for Operation Mascara were inadequate and that, in any case, the justification for the aborted mission had from its inception been fictional. Based on the flimsy evidence submitted, there was no justification for the elaborate manoeuvres to entrap an agent suspected of treason.

Moreover, certain allies in the Western intelligence universe [cynics assumed this a reference to Israeli intelligence] had, for their own reasons, muddied the waters of what could have provided a legitimate reason for the initial probe.

Nobody really understood these deliberately obscure observations. But the bottom line, as echoed through the windowless corridors of MI6's home base, was that the commissioners of inquiry had put the best face on a failed and unjustified mission to entrap an innocent officer of the service.

No names came to the surface, but the cognoscenti murmured that Department B3's days were numbered. What that unconventional group of agents and subagents had achieved over the years [admittedly quite a lot] could now be replicated by the head office, particularly by the long-established but newly invigorated Mideast and North Africa desk, where staffing had been increased exponentially.

But was this the end of the story? Had the lessons of the twentieth century been learned and applied? In the scandal-ridden days of Philby, Blunt, Blake, Burgess, and Mclean, Britain's unfettered press exposed the incompetence, negligence, and laxity of London's spymasters. This had to be stopped. What happens in Vauxhall Cross and outposts like Gower Street should stay within the sedate confines of the nation's intelligence and security networks.

But the members of the press, especially those who dedicated themselves to uncovering political and government scandals of one sort or another, soon detected that something was rotten on the south bank of the Thames. The distinct odor of scandal, incompetence, and cover-up lingered over the news desks and editorial conferences of the nation's leading broadsheets, tabloids, and internet news sites.

Accusations of scandal, cover-up, and conspiracy led the front pages for several weeks. Teams from the tabloid press were sent to the Black Dog on eighteen-hour shifts in an attempt to scrape up some scoop-worthy crumbs of information.

At Westminster, the prime minister and an assortment of front bench cabinet ministers faced an onslaught of probing questions from the opposition Labour Party and its new leader, Jeremy Corbyn.

But to this date, no credible witness to history has emerged.

* * *

Within a few weeks of what became known internally as the 'B3 debacle,' Sir Percy Bolton, director general of MI6, was delighted to reassure his old friend Sir Nigel Adair that he had full confidence in the new anti-leak measures that had been implemented on his lengthy watch. The need for total, watertight security in all matters related to their clandestine activities, everyday routine chores, and critical operations, had been finally inculcated into the mindset of his diverse staff, from top to bottom.

'But there's one thing that still worries me, a kind of chink in our armor,' Sir Percy said, after the first swig of his usual pink gin aperitif.

'Please elaborate,' Sir Nigel said, concerned.

'Our Mr. Michael Vaux.'

'He's retired now. You know that,' Sir Nigel said dismissively.

'Exactly. He might, out of unwanted *and* unwonted idleness, just get the itch to write his story. The peg would be the terrible treatment meted out by us—the unfounded suspicions we nursed about his loyalties, the frame-up engineered by your department. You know what the tabloids would make of that. The bloody story would refuse to die. It could go on for months.'

Sir Nigel sipped his Madeira as he composed his response.

'Well, we can't control everything. But on my last meeting with him, I did warn him of the dire consequences if he breached the Official Secrets Act.' As an afterthought, he added, 'Plus he was paid a hefty compensation package to stay mum. I don't think he'd want to risk losing that.'

'Oh, well. We'll keep our fingers crossed.'

The two Knights of the Realm then embarked on their regular, weekly lunch which usually lasted until the end of the working day.

Chapter 27

Michael Vaux, back in his sprawling bungalow in Hertfordshire, was as mad as hell at the ruse perpetrated against him by Craw, whom he called a creep to his face and to anyone else who cared to listen. The Mossad's motivations were more understandable, given his known sympathies for the Palestinians in their struggle for a permanent homeland.

His anger was in large part assuaged by the receipt of the initially promised remuneration for taking a lead part in the ill-starred Operation Mascara; plus, thanks to the efforts of Sir Nigel, additional compensation, equal to twice the promised basic remuneration, for being wrongfully suspected of treason, as well as for the grave encroachments on his privacy perpetrated by the spy agency via the talents of trainee Patrick Thursfield.

Vaux was hardly dismayed to learn that Alan Craw had been ordered to take a six-month leave of absence without pay and that the Israelis, after much soul-searching, had decided to let sleeping dogs lie.

Thus, thought Vaux, do Britain's spymasters avoid damaging publicity about their foibles, misdeeds, and miscalculations.

Now here he was, a few weeks to go before Christmas, back in his quiet residential street, the quotidian boredom of which was offset by the bucolic view of Hertfordshire's rolling farmland to the south towards London, long evenings playing Duke Ellington's 1930s hits—and by the close proximity of the Pig & Whistle, his local watering hole.

On this particular morning, he was waiting for Anne, who had rented a car from London Heathrow and was at this very minute heading north-west on the M1. They had talked to each other on the phone, and Anne had promised to tell him the whole story. She was referring to her long and obdurate silence during her enforced absence in Berlin, where she had somehow launched a promising career in the Diplomatic Corps. To keep her happy and pliant, she had been appointed a probationary deputy assistant in the passport and visa department of Her Majesty's Foreign Service.

He heard the rumble of a car's engine as a black Audi A4 drew up in the gravel driveway. She was slimmer, and her blonde hair fell casually around her shoulders. They hugged each other for several minutes. She was crying but tried to hide it by snuggling up to him so they were both looking past each other, the long parting having created a sort of unfamiliar shyness.

Two or three weeks of romantic bliss; reminiscences; reverence towards her recently departed father; a few trips to the Pig; and some not-so-successful attempts by Anne to cook Vaux a traditional British Sunday lunch. He was in paradise.

But then came the knock on the door. Vaux looked puzzled and left Anne in the kitchen, stirring scrambled eggs with a long wooden spoon.

He opened the front door. Before him stood Alena, her long hair radiant in the early morning sun, big round sunglasses hiding her deep brown eyes. She was smiling the way Vaux had always remembered.

'Alena, darling! What brings you to this neck of the woods?' He wrapped his arms around her shoulders. He saw she had parked her rented Ford behind Anne's Audi.

'Nice to see you again, Michael. I've been planning to call on you for some time. It won't take long.'

'Good, good. Of course, I've heard the incredibly convoluted story. I can't wait to hear your version of everything. But that can all wait. Anne's here, and she's in the kitchen preparing breakfast. Would you like something? A coffee?'

'No, thank you. This won't take long, darling. I'm due at the airport in about an hour, so I want to get this over with.'

Vaux adopted a theatrical look of shock. 'But you've just arrived.'

'Yes, I know.'

Vaux then saw Alena's hand reach into her black leather Gucci handbag. He saw the glint of a small Glock 43, the barrel elongated by a suppressor. She was pointing it at his chest.

'What the hell?'

Alena Hussein shot Michael Vaux three times in the chest at very short range.

He fell back on the ceramic-tiled floor, a fountain of blood springing from his collapsed chest.

Alena heard a clatter of pots and pans from the kitchen. She turned quickly and rushed back to the rented Ford Fiesta. As she backed out of the driveway, she caught a glimpse of a blonde girl crouching over a lifeless body, screaming in disbelief, despair, and denial.

* * *

Nobody knew exactly what happened next. But Gerald Dawson, who had returned to his workaday world of running the Bar du Port and caretaking a deserted SIS safe house, was told several months later by one of his shadowy contacts that Michael Vaux's assailant, after the dirty deed was perpetrated, had hightailed it to Heathrow's Terminal 4. There she was met by two delighted officials from the Syrian embassy who, after a few celebratory drinks in the first-class lounge, put her on the next Aeroflot flight to Moscow. From there, she took a connecting Syria Air flight back to war-torn Damascus.

Twenty-four hours later, news of Alena Hussein's re-defection spread like wildfire in the quiet corridors of London's spy establishment. In coordination with Department B3, MI6 embarked on one of the longest and deepest counter-intelligence probes since the Philby fiasco, seeking to discover what went wrong. Why was Alena Hussein's story so readily believed? Who and where were the fact checkers?

Old and experienced hands claimed that the Syrian side had planted a mole, probably a decade or so ago, who worked on the Mideast and North Africa desk. Hussein's handler/controller had to be located within the buttressed walls of the Vauxhall fortress. But the search for this elusive double agent, despite Bill Oxley's herculean efforts, had so far produced nothing conclusive.

At first, suspicions were centred on Doug Bradford, who had headed up the Mideast desk for just two years. But Alena Hussein's long-term deception clearly extended far beyond his ascendancy. Sir Percival Bolton, who had headed the spy agency for over fifteen years, offered to aid the investigators by going through the personnel files of every man and woman recruited under his watch. But Bradford rejected this approach. The crisis centred on the Mideast desk, and the top Mideast personnel would handle it.

The investigation into Alena Hussein's long-term and effective betrayals continues to this day. Her intelligence reports over the years have been scrutinized microscopically. In the final analysis, they presented a stream of chicken feed, sparsely punctuated by the odd piece of useful intelligence that Damascus had decided would not affect the attainment of its political and military goals.

The only sure fact is that in the murky annals of the world's secret intelligence services, Alena Hussein has been universally but reluctantly awarded the dubious honour as the longest serving triple agent in the history of espionage.

Meanwhile, the ripple effects of the intelligence disaster spread far and wide. For no good reason Gerald Dawson could think of, Bruno Valayer, Syria's stylish honorary consul in Marseille, France's second biggest city, became a regular patron of the enigmatic and discreet bar in the cobblestone alleyway, a few yards from the edge of the old harbour.

Notes

Note 1: See *The Spy and the Traitor* by Ben Macintyre [2018].

Note 2: The infamous 'Cambridge Five' were Kim Philby, Donald Maclean, Guy Burgess, Anthony Blunt, and John Cairncross—all graduates of Cambridge University.

Note 3: The biggest spy scandal in British history involved the stealthy defections of Burgess and Maclean by night ferry to Ostende and then by car [?] to Moscow. Both men had worked at the British embassy in Washington. And later, the uncovering of their friend Philby, a former journalist, who quickly left Beirut [where he worked as a correspondent for the *Economist*] for points east. Cairncross, the fifth man, was never brought to trial and lived his life out in the south of France.

Note 4: The Directorate General for External Security [DGSE] is the French equivalent of Britain's MI6 and America's CIA.

Note 5: After the Six Day War, Israel won control of the West Bank, East Jerusalem, Gaza, and Syria's Golan Heights.

Note 6: In 1973, Egyptian and Syrian forces invaded Israeli-occupied Sinai and the Golan Heights. Israel, with US help, pushed the Arab armies back. The conflict was resolved by the Camp David accords of 1978. The Sinai was returned to Egypt.

Note 7: 'Pavement artist' is a term coined by John le Carré to describe those whose work in the world of espionage centres on surreptitiously following people [suspected agents, for example] and generally spying on their activities in order to report their movements and habits.

Note 8: Syria's General Security Directorate [GSD] oversees internal and external intelligence services. Equivalent to MI5/MI6 in the UK.

Note 9: The Rue de Fauberg du Temple and the adjacent streets that lead north-east from the Place de la Republique to the Canal-St. Martin area bore the brunt of the terrorist shootings that shook Paris on the evening of November 13, 2015. In total, the terrorists killed 113 victims. A small concrete memorial has been erected on the nearby corner of the Rue St. Maur to some of the local victims of that tragic episode.

Note 10: The Australian Secret Intelligence Service [ASIS]. Established in 1952, headquartered in Canberra, Australia.

Note 11: The Black Dog is a pub in Vauxhall, London, located in a backstreet off the Thames embankment. It is frequented by SIS staff, from secretaries to top bureaucrats.

Printed in the United States
By Bookmasters